D1133538

Murder, Honey

A Carol Sabala Mystery

Vinnie Hansen

Murder, Honey
A Carol Sabala Mystery

Copyright © 2014 Vinnie Hansen.

All rights reserved.

Published by: Misterio Press
www.misteriopress.com

No part of this book may be reproduced, scanned, or distributed in any printed or electronic form without express written permission from the publisher. The scanning, uploading, and distribution of this book via the internet or any other means without the permission of the publisher is illegal and punishable by law. Please do not participate in or encourage piracy of copyrighted materials in violation of the author's rights. Purchase only authorized editions.

This is a work of fiction. Names, characters, businesses, places, events and incidents are either the products of the author's imagination or used in a fictitious manner. Any resemblance to actual persons, living or dead, or actual events is purely coincidental.

ISBN-13: 978-0-9913208-3-7

ISBN-10: 0991320832

Cover design and book layout: Book Cover Corner, www.bookcovercorner.com
Background cover artwork: Daniel S. Friedman

"Death in the Open" copyright © 1973 by the Massachuetts Medical Society, from THE LIVES OF A CELL by Lewis Thomas. Used with permission from Viking Penguin, a division of Penguin Putnam Inc.

Hansen, Vinnie.

Murder, Honey / Vinnie Hansen. — 2nd ed.

To Daniel Stuart Friedman, my husband

PRAISE FOR HANSEN'S WORK

"I love Carol Sabala…quirky, gutsy and my kind of gal in an aqua tank top."
—Cara Black, author of the Aimée Leduc mystery series

"In Sabala, Hansen has created a likable sleuth whose many problems readers may readily identify with."
—Michael Cornelius, *The Bloomsbury Review*

"Hansen's sense of humor and protagonist make for a good read. I particularly enjoyed her faithfully rendered Santa Cruz background."
—Laura Crum, author of the Gail McCarthy murder mystery series

"With edgy precision, Hansen applies all the elements of a good mystery: interesting plot, compelling characters, a finely drawn sense of place, and excellent writing."
—Denise Osborne, author of Feng Shui Mysteries and Queenie Davilov Mysteries

"Art, Wine, & Bullets *is a delightful, appealing, and delectable read."*
—Midwest Book Review

ALSO BY VINNIE HANSEN:

One Tough Cookie

Rotten Dates

Tang Is Not Juice

Death with Dessert

Art, Wine & Bullets

1991

CHAPTER ONE

"Be careful what you wish for, Carol," my mom always said. "It might come true."

What happened with Head Chef Jean Alcee Fortier was a case in point. I had wished him dead a dozen times, and I remember one of those times vividly. I'd stumbled into Archibald's at three-thirty a.m. in a semi-somnolent state. Even after years of working as a baker at this swanky restaurant, I hadn't adjusted to the early morning hours.

I entered the building from the loading dock, which was on the front of the building, but well screened from the brick U where uniformed valets would later hustle to park Mercedes and BMW's.

A forty-watt bulb illuminated the time clock. This was one of the kitchen manager's subtle manipulations, to make us squint, and therefore to focus, on what we were doing. People underestimated Eldon. The bumbling, mild-mannered Clark Kent exterior hid his cunning interior. He projected a sense of incompetence while all the hard evidence suggested otherwise. For one thing, he'd held on to his job for ten years in Santa Cruz, one of the most competitive towns in the world for eating establishments. Secondly, the kitchen made a profit for the conference center.

The hall lights were off, but I knew the place like my home.

I was groggier than usual. Chad had awakened me at midnight with a cough he'd recently developed. Just as his deep breaths lulled me back to sleep, a cough lodged in the middle, like a skip in a record. I turned on the lamp and shook him awake. Even half asleep, he was a hunk, but that didn't stop my irritation.

His blue-green eyes gradually comprehended the situation and glinted with annoyance. "You woke me up to tell me that I was coughing."

"You're keeping me awake."

"Go sleep on the couch."

"You go sleep on the couch," I retorted. "You're the one who's choosing to commit suicide with cigarettes."

He fell asleep and I ended up on the couch.

Between the hard cushions and my angry mood, I hadn't slept at all, and I entered the fluorescent glare of the locker room in a sleepwalking state. Not that many years ago, the female employees had changed clothes in the tiny restroom, while the male employees enjoyed the convenience of the locker room. Then this last bastion of chauvinism had been converted to a unisex facility with a screened section in each of the far corners.

I didn't see Fortier at first, but he certainly had seen me, and made no attempt to cover himself. More naked than Adam, he sat on a bench in front of the lockers.

I gasped.

"Thank you," he said, in a voice like black velvet and old whiskey. "I know I'm good-looking, but I don't inspire many gasps." He smiled, a wicked, relishing grin, his white teeth set off by olive skin. At 3:30 in the morning and stark naked, he looked impeccably groomed, his black, wavy hair recently barbered and brushed straight back. He stood, revealing the works: broad shoulders, washboard stomach, and a penis to match his ego.

"Excuse me." I backed out, my cheeks burning, more with anger than embarrassment. I should have known decorum was a wasted effort.

"Hey, Carol, don't go. My sausage needs some spice."

I went outside the building to cool down. The asshole. Why did all the women flip over him? Given the image only now fading from my retinas, that was a rhetorical question. I understood how his new girlfriend, the twenty-year-old Delores, mistook his low-life humor for charm, but how could mature women like Suzanne or Concepción take inconsideration as *joie de vivre*? With the right looks, a person could get away with murder.

On the loading dock, I faced the grounds of the conference center and inhaled the jasmine and eucalyptus-scented darkness. Archibald's was on a wooded hill, high above fog-shrouded Santa Cruz. The serenity soothed me.

I wondered what Fortier was doing here so early, although, he often was the second person to arrive. I begrudgingly acknowledged that he was deserving of his position as Head Chef, and wondered if a sexual harassment complaint would cost me my job. In truth, I was pissed partly because I'd been too startled to think of a snappy comeback.

As I paced the concrete dock, waiting for someone else to arrive, I had one of those momentary epiphanies where I understood completely why my husband Chad smoked. I wanted a cigarette and I hadn't smoked since high school.

Looking back, I suppose I waited out there getting chilled because I expected the next arrival to be my buddy and comforter, Buzz Fraser. Instead, I heard a motorcycle roar through the night. Unlike the rest of us who parked a half-mile away and stumbled to the kitchen, Patsy drove her Harley right up to the dumpster.

"Hey, kiddo, whatcha doing out here?" her disembodied voice said. Patsy routinely wore black leather, so I couldn't see her, only the winking red reflector on her helmet.

"Oh," I said, "I'm contemplating how to kill a son-of-a-bitch."

Another thing my mom used to say was "hold your tongue." When she'd say that, I'd stick out my tongue and grab it to prove that I was the impossible, incorrigible kid that she claimed.

Little did I know that I was about to develop a keen appreciation for my mom's clichés, especially the one about being careful what you wished for.

CHAPTER TWO

I didn't have an opportunity to vent to Buzz until my break. I ran into him in the Employees Dining Room, or the EDR as all the employees called it. I smelled his vanilla scent come up behind me as I was getting a cup of coffee. He gave my long auburn braid of hair a playful tug.

When I turned around, he took one look at me and said, "What's wrong?"

"Fortier."

"That explains everything." He poured a cup of coffee for himself. Blue eyes over prominent cheekbones dominated Buzz's face, and complete understanding registered in them as he nodded toward a table in the corner.

We sat at the table, and I recounted the incident.

Buzz patted my hand. He could get away with that because I knew he was too honorable to make a move on a married woman. "I can think of a few good recipes with sausage."

I grinned but noticed hardness in his eyes. Buzz had reasons for hating for Fortier—not that I'd had any luck persuading him to talk about it. "He certainly shafted you," I said. "No pun intended."

Buzz offered a grim smile. He took a sip of coffee and glanced around the empty room. He ran his fingers along his square jaw line. He was as attractive as Fortier, although neither was conventionally handsome. "This coffee is weak."

He wasn't going to bite at my gambit. His unpretentious calm could be infuriating.

"Are you ever going to tell me what happened with the show?"

He sighed, crossed his left arm over his chef's smock, and used it to prop his hoisting arm.

My heart felt a tug and ache for Buzz Fraser. He was hands down my favorite person at work. He rubbed aloe on my burns and told me Chad was a lucky man. All of us had expected him to star on a new cooking program on local television. And he'd been eager to share the limelight. He'd proposed that I appear to make breads and Suzanne guest star to prepare salads. But somehow Fortier had usurped Buzz's program, and Buzz refused to discuss what had happened.

Anger bubbled to the surface of my skin like water about to boil. "To hell with just the sausage," I said. "We should cook up a nice hearty stew."

Buzz shook his head. He'd left his chef's hat in the kitchen and powder-fine, blond hair puffed away from his scalp. He looked past me to the blank wall. "Leave it alone, Carol."

My anger switched toward him. "Leave it alone? How am I

supposed to leave *it* alone? I don't even know what *it* is."

Buzz slipped his empty cup inside mine. "I've moved on," he said, standing up. "There's nothing that can be done, anyway."

I snatched the sleeve of his smock. "Nothing that can be done?" My voice rose. I was not a person born to accept injustice. "There's always something that can be done." He twisted away so hard, my grip on his smock leveraged me out of the plastic chair. I let go of the fabric. "You could confront Fortier. You could sabotage his food prep. Blow up the television station." My face was hot.

Buzz spun toward me and placed a hand on each shoulder. "Shhhhh. I love you, Carol, but let it go."

He gave me a peck on the cheek, wheeled, and strode into the hallway. He wasn't quick enough. I saw the sheen of tears in his eyes.

Two weeks later, on a hot summer day, which in Santa Cruz meant in the eighties, Patsy, Suzanne and I gathered and laughed over beer as we hatched progressively nastier ways to kill Fortier.

I'd met up with my two co-workers at a sports bar with a big screen television to watch the first episode of the cooking program, Cruz'n Cuisine.

"A cooking show?" The bartender thunked our beers on the counter. "This is a sports bar."

And what a stupid idea that was. People kept opening them because they were trendy and the places kept folding. No one grasped that Santa Cruz was not Cleveland or Detroit. We had no home team, no unifying mania, no fans to sit in an empty, freezing stadium to watch away-games on screens.

"Let's pound these and go to my house to watch," I suggested.

"But we'll miss the opening," Suzanne said.

Patsy planted her elbows on the bar and leaned over the dark wood into the bartender's square face. "I know what kind of bar it is." Patsy had a body that should have drawn an admiring glance. Jutting toward the young man were breasts one usually saw only in magazines. However, the bartender eyed her shaved head with the poof of mauve curls at the front, the ears riddled with rings, the tattoo on her bicep, and the burn scars all kitchen workers have. Biceps popped below Patsy's black muscle shirt. These details distracted him.

Patsy added in a gruff, but reasonable voice, "If anyone comes in and wants sports, you can put on sports."

The man's dark eyes looked around the room. We were the only customers in the joint except for a man in his thirties with a conservative haircut and a tailored suit, an anomaly for Santa Cruz.

"Customers come first," Suzanne said sweetly.

As the bartender inspected her, he underwent a transformation. His shoulders dropped, his mouth relaxed, his eyes softened.

Suzanne looked like a cream puff, with golden, sun-kissed skin exposed by a sleeveless, flowered dress. Permed, frizzy blond hair was banded into the topping.

"KRUZ channel?" he asked.

"Thank you," Suzanne said. "I'll buy you a beer."

I guess this was what my mom meant when she said, "You can get more flies with honey than vinegar." My reply had always been, "God, Ma, who wants more flies?"

The bartender agreed to let Suzanne buy him a Coke, and

then, to his credit, drank it at the other end of the bar as he leaned over a newspaper.

The program started at four. The title scrolled across the screen and then our sexist Head Chef Jean Fortier waved as bright music played and the camera zoomed in. Fortier wore what looked like a uniform from Archibald's: white smock and chef's hat.

"What's Eldon going to think of the uniform?" I wondered aloud. Eldon was a born bureaucrat, the kind who counted towels and uniforms. He would have counted beans had Archibald's served anything so humble.

"Eldon probably supplied the uniform in exchange for a plug," Patsy said.

I had to agree. That sounded like Eldon. "Is this filmed in his own kitchen?"

"Yeah." Suzanne clamped her lips and a blush spread up her neck.

Suzanne was sweet, built like a Barbie doll, and had once dated Fortier, which may have qualified her as a "dumb blonde." But she wasn't. Under the spray of frizz, lively brown eyes checked out the world. Of all Fortier's formers, she'd been on the most equal footing. She had an AA in Culinary Arts and Hospitality from Cabrillo College and was anxious to move up the ladder. She'd used Fortier for advancement as much as he'd used her for sex. Ironically, it had been Suzanne's promotion to head of the *garde manger* that had opened the door for Eldon to hire Delores Medina, Fortier's latest pursuit. According to kitchen lore, Fortier had once, long before my time, romanced Esperanza Medina, Delores's mother. The kitchen was a regular Melrose Place. But Suzanne showed none of the ire of a woman scorned.

She'd gotten what she wanted.

On the screen, Fortier flashed a brilliant mouthful of straight white teeth and modestly introduced himself as the King of Cuisine. "Everybody loves something sweet, dahlin'," he said, laying on his New Orleans accent. "Especially me." He winked.

"The pig," Patsy muttered.

The man in the gray, pinstriped suit watched the program from his table. The bartender looked up worriedly from the sports section, but the guy didn't make any indication he'd rather see baseball.

"Today I'll show you how to whip up a special delicacy—*oeufs a la neige*," our gorgeous Jean Alcee Fortier continued. "Don't worry. It's easier to make than to pronounce." I could imagine women around the county tuning in for the eye candy. He could whip up tuna salad for all they cared. He turned a careful profile to the camera as he poured milk into a chicken fryer.

"If Buzz had gotten the show, that could be you up there, Patsy," I murmured, even as I wondered if that were true. Would a local station air someone as radical looking as Patsy?

"Hey, bartender," Patsy called.

He raised his head from the newspaper.

"Got any darts?"

He ignored her, looking back at the sheets spread on the counter.

Fortier spelled the name of the dessert, a rather nice touch, I thought, in spite of my anger. Note to self, spell Sabala for people right off. On the phone, people assumed I'd said Zavala, and in fairness Sabala was a corruption of that name. People didn't make this assumption when they met me face to face, as I didn't look Mexican, or even the half-Mexican I was.

"Another name is 'floating island' because we'll create little islands of meringue in a delectable custard. In N' Awlins, we make this as a birthday treat."

"I bet he'll be able to sell his cookbook now," Suzanne said.

Patsy and I exchanged blank looks over her golden head. We hadn't known anything about a cookbook. Because Chef Fortier behaved stupidly, it was easy to forget that he was talented and capable.

"Why did you want to watch him on the big screen?" Suzanne teased Patsy, insinuating that even she might be vulnerable to his charms.

Patsy snorted. "He wouldn't fit on a little one."

"Poor Buzz," I said. "I wonder if he's watching."

"Why torture himself?" Patsy chugged the last of her Red Hook as Fortier separated eggs with expertise. "If I were Buzz, I'd kill the asshole."

"Yeah," Suzanne said dreamily, eyes locked on the screen, apparently stripping Fortier to his full glory, as I'd seen him two weeks earlier.

The memory of the locker room incident fueled a fire in my gut. Later that day, Fortier had backed me into a corner of the kitchen and breathed into my ear, "A little too much for you?"

"Why," I'd whispered back, "does a guy with a gorgeous girlfriend, young enough to assuage any mid-life crisis, need to harass a thirty-something, married woman?"

The word "harass" backed him off about an inch. He

smirked, raised a perfect, thick eyebrow, and stretched one arm to the wall. Even in a chef's jacket and even with my anger, there was no denying his musky masculinity. He exuded pheromones like a skunk.

I slugged him in the breadbasket.

Fortier emitted a satisfying grunt and released the arm.

Victor, the dishwasher, dropped a huge, stainless steel bowl on the tile. "Ow, *a la chingada.*" As the bowl spun and rang, I slithered past Fortier.

He grabbed my arm. "If you even think sexual harassment, forget it. I'll get you for assault. I have a witness," he hissed. "You don't."

Suzanne nudged my shoulder and brought me back to the reality of the sports bar. "Buzz should make some preserves and not quite cook them enough," Suzanne said jokingly. "If he left them in the kitchen, the King of Cuisine would taste them sooner or later." It was a strain for Suzanne to be so "bad," but she wanted to fit in with the crowd.

"Sooner," Patsy said. Fortier was famous for sampling and critiquing.

"Botulism is not a reliable vehicle. Even if you canned sloppily, you wouldn't be guaranteed botulism, and there's no way of knowing whether you've produced it or not, short of testing the stuff on your cat."

The bartender, who'd slid down the counter to check on us, stared at me, as did Patsy and Suzanne. It wasn't botulism, but me that fascinated them, much as a squished bug might.

"Don't you know murder is my hobby?"

"Tell us the best way to do it. How would you kill Fortier?" Patsy rubbed her hands together and cut her eyes toward the bartender with a smirk on her face.

Beyond Patsy's shoulder, the suited man raptly watched the program. He extracted a black leather organizer and a gold pen from his jacket.

For a moment I imagined using Fortier's head as a volleyball, but Patsy hadn't asked for the most satisfying method, she'd asked for the "best." I assumed that meant a successful way that would avoid detection. "Poison." I was a lightweight drinker and felt buzzed as I started my second beer. "Take Empress Wu, who rose from a concubine to be the only female leader in the history of China. If her husband so much as looked at another woman, the woman had a way of dying after dinner, didn't matter if it was her sister or her daughter."

My audience had lost interest in the program. Three sets of eyes gazed at me. I rarely had a chance to hold forth on my favorite topic, so I continued, a little disappointed that I hadn't snared the interest of the suited man.

"Then there's Agrippina, who killed Claudius by feeding him a mushroom from her plate. Or, for a serious alchemist, take the Marquise de Brinvilliers. She tested her stuff on children in a charity hospital."

Suzanne wrinkled her nose. "That's awful."

"Well, she must have perfected the art, because when she went to nurse her ill father, she slowly poisoned him to death, and he was so unaware of the connection that he thanked her for her care with his dying breath."

"Gives me the willies." Suzanne pulled a pink scrunchie from her hair, shook the blond frizz down and then pulled the spray up and re-banded it, so it looked more or less as it had before.

"Oh," Patsy said, "you ever seen *I, Claudius*?" I could tell this was gang-up-to-gross-out Suzanne, a common kitchen pastime. "I can understand why Agrippina killed that idiot." Her face took on a meditative look. "Murder was probably the only way women could gain power in those days."

"Well," I said, "going back to the original question, given the overworked state of the police and the burden of proving guilt beyond a reasonable doubt, it's easier to get away with murder than books or movies would have you believe. Especially if you use poison and plan."

"Sorry to interrupt."

Patsy and Suzanne jumped, but I'd seen Mr. Slick moving toward us. What he lacked in height, he made up for with tailoring. The suit was well cut and he looked like money down to his supple, Italian loafers.

"I noticed that you seem to know this chef." Dark, all-business eyes glanced at the screen. "He's very good. He's a natural in front of the camera, and with his looks and that accent, he'll make the female audience swoon."

Patsy and I swapped looks of amusement since neither of us was in need of smelling salts.

"Who are you?" she asked.

From the leather organizer he slipped out a card and plunked it on the counter. His name was less important than the curly black words: Exploration Channel, Programming Acquisition and Development.

CHAPTER THREE

Before trying to drive, Suzanne, Patsy and I walked to the nearby Carpo's to put food in our stomachs. Carpo's was a noisy family restaurant featuring some of the best fries anywhere and slabs of homemade pie.

I called Chad to let him know I'd go from the restaurant to my volleyball class. I kept shorts, my old athletic shoes, and kneepads in my car: clear signs of an addict.

"I hope you don't plan to go poking your nose into Fortier's business," Chad said. I'd given him an abbreviated version of my run-in with Fortier, and Chad knew that I'd met with "the girls" to watch the show, but his remark still seemed to come for no discernible reason.

"I beg your pardon." I slathered on the indignation to make sure he heard it over the background clatter of trays and noisy children. Even though it came from left field, I understood Chad's insinuation. I did want to know how Fortier had landed Buzz's show. Depending on the person asked, I was nosy or curious, stubborn or persistent.

"Have you been drinking?" Chad asked.

"Only two beers."

"I hope you aren't driving."

"Not at the moment."

Chad sighed.

I didn't think drinking and driving was a joking matter, either, but my husband's attitude annoyed me.

"Are you sure you should go to volleyball?"

I sighed, reassured him I would be fine, and went to join Patsy and Suzanne who had reached the front of the line. They had drawn the eyes of every man who could look without craning from a booth or getting socked by his wife. It didn't hurt when I joined them. My hair tumbled down my back, accenting my strong, five-foot-eight build. I wasn't as cute as Suzanne or as striking as Patsy, but I could hold my own somewhere in the middle ground.

The three of us spent an hour eating, speculating about Mr. Slick's business card and what it could mean for Fortier, and lamenting that the opportunity hadn't befallen Buzz.

"But if it were Buzz," Suzanne said, "the guy might not have been interested. He specifically mentioned Jean's sex appeal."

"Don't you think Buzz is sexy?" I asked, nibbling the end of a substantial fry and challenging the two women across the table.

Patsy's muscled arms moved into an elaborate, palms-up shrug and the dragon on her bicep moved, shooting out its flame. "Sexy? Penises are the most ridiculous-looking things in the world. How can anything so obvious be erotic?"

"There's more to men than their penises," I snapped. Patsy's male bashing could get tiring.

"Tell them that." She took another big bite of burger. In spite of all her effort to look like a self-proclaimed "dyke," Patsy's creamy, oval face remained doe-like.

I looked at Suzanne.

She stopped mid forkful of salad and squirmed in the vinyl booth. "What?"

"Do you think Buzz is sexy?" I suspected Suzanne had shifted her affection to my friend, although Buzz didn't believe it. Working around Fortier had obliterated his sense of his own sex appeal.

"A little," Suzanne said. She put down her fork and rearranged her hair. "Not like Jean."

"Thank God he's not like Jean," Patsy muttered. "He's an asshole." She used both hands to pick up her burger, and let a trickle of juice run down her forearm.

"Do either of you know how Fortier got that show instead of Buzz?" I asked, steering the conversation away from Patsy's impending diatribe. I wondered, not for the first time, what had made her so bitter.

They both shrugged. "Geez, I thought if anybody would know, it would be you," Suzanne said.

"When I've asked about it, Buzz mutters and says Fortier is an asshole."

"See," Patsy crowed. "Buzz agrees with me."

"Everybody agrees with you," I said.

"Being an asshole runs in the family," Patsy said. "I hate Fortier's little twit niece, too."

"Alexis?" I hardly knew the girl because she worked the afternoon shift, but Patsy had to deal with her as part of the pastry department.

"She's sweet." Suzanne shivered. The summer evenings cooled fast with incoming fog, and apparently the crowd and steam from the kitchen were not enough to warm her fragile shoulders.

"If you don't mind room temperature I.Q.'s." Patsy wiped her face and threw a wadded napkin onto the center of the table. "Uncle Jean this, and Uncle Jean that," Patsy mimicked. "She acts like Fortier's a fuckin' god. She's been in pastry like four months and the other day she starts telling me how to improve my mousse."

"You said yourself that she's parroting Fortier." I used my most pacifying voice. Patsy in a full-scale rant was not a pretty sight.

"No doubt. People are idiots." Patsy rose from the booth. "Present company excepted."

"You know, we could just not give the business card to Fortier," I said.

Suzanne's expression made me feel ashamed of myself.

Later, as I drove my '66 Karmann Ghia to volleyball class, I combed through everything Buzz had said about the cooking show, which took about one minute.

I drove past Gayle's bakery, which held no temptation for me. I spent five mornings a week with my nose encrusted with flour, invaded by the smells of sour dough baguettes, apple muffins, and snickerdoodles. The aroma from the bakery simply reminded me of work, and watching the cooking show had stirred up old questions. Chad's comment about my nosiness held something akin to foresight.

I parked in the nearly full lot of the New Brighton Middle School gym and climbed out into the chilly mist. My mother used to call me Carol Cat; she also frequently reminded me that curiosity killed the cat. The admonishment had done nothing to deter me, and I was fully alive at last report.

As I approached the double door, a pack of middle-aged people in shorts and sweats, their faces and hair damp, poured from the gym. But there were still plenty of people playing volleyball. I entered the comforting embrace of sweat and dust and reverberating noise.

A volleyball bounced toward me across the wood floor. How had Fortier usurped Buzz's show? I scooped up the ball and tossed it to its owner. I planned to find out.

CHAPTER FOUR

For the next couple of weeks, I steered my conversations with Buzz toward the cooking show, using my most skillful interview techniques.

He coughed up nothing.

After one of our breaks, he heaved a huge sigh, grasped both of my shoulders and said, "Carol, you have to stop pestering me about this."

And I realized I did, or I might lose a friend.

So, I concentrated on questioning my co-workers. Eventually I had to concede that no one knew squat, although rumors abounded.

"He must have bribed someone," Patsy offered.

"He bedded the woman in charge," Todd, the back-line cook, said.

"A woman was in charge?"

"I dunno."

The riddle of how Fortier stole Buzz's show gnawed at me for months. Unable to solve it, I invented scenarios that flamed my dislike of Fortier. So, when he pulled a mini stepladder over to my bakery and plopped down, my first thought was to escape his presence, even though he looked waxen and woozy. He even sat down, which was unlike him.

I didn't stick around to see what was wrong. "Gotta help Esperanza with a wedding cake." I hustled over to pastry, hoping that he didn't get sick in the bakery.

A few minutes later, when Patsy grabbed Head Chef Jean Alcee Fortier's raven hair and hoisted his face from my *lebkuchen* dough, I uncharitably thought that even half dead the man remained a pain in the ass. Fortier's body fell heavily against Patsy. She and Todd lowered him to the tiled floor near the dishwashers.

Eldon waddled rapidly, like a prodded duck, to the hall phone to call 911.

A crowd of kitchen workers jammed the hallway outside my bakery. "Is he breathing?" asked Delores Medina. Tears welled in her blue eyes. Esperanza, her mother, stood behind her with a hand on either shoulder.

Todd pressed two fingers to Jean Alcee Fortier's carotid artery. "I don't feel anything. Can anyone here help me with CPR?"

"Yo." Patsy knelt down. She pushed back Fortier's chin, probed his mouth with her fingers, and breathed into the body while Todd worked his chest like bread dough.

The sight of Patsy putting her lips to the bloodless ones of Fortier was nearly as astonishing as his yellow, apparently dead body.

Delores stifled a sob.

"*Pobrecita.*" Esperanza tried to turn her daughter to her breast, but the girl stared, transfixed, at the man on the floor.

Eldon returned from the phone and grumped. "What was he doing here? He was supposed to go home sick. This is just what we need, for a known chef to die in our kitchen. How is that going to look?"

"*El Punetero*," Victor muttered. Everyone but Eldon knew he'd been called The Masturbator, but no one smiled.

"He's breathing!" Delores cried.

"No, *mija*," Esperanza said. "That's Patsy's breath causing the movemen'." Esperanza's accent was heavy enough to make her both sexy and hard to understand.

Eldon fluttered nervously at the perimeter of the group. He patted his hands together. "Come on, you guys. Everyone but Patsy and Todd, back to your stations. We have a kitchen to run." Eldon was the only one among us who could manage a kitchen with a dead man on the floor. I guessed that was how a six-foot-two dumpling became an executive chef: Buzz was a better cook and Fortier was more flamboyant.

We dispersed reluctantly. I heard the sirens shrieking up the wooded hill from the hospital, a convenient mile away.

"Oh, good Jesus, sirens." Eldon puttered nervously to the back line where Ray had returned to work. He lifted the lid of the lunch soup *du jour*—vichyssoise—that Todd had been preparing. He ladled up a sample, blew on it, and delicately slurped.

"Todd needs to season it," Ray said.

"I can tell," Eldon said.

I stepped around the body, back to my table, and looked at

the huge pan of brown, spicy dough for the *lebkuchen*, a Christmas honey cake that I baked as individual cookies. Fortier must have been sick. I wondered if he had sampled my dough, anyway. It would be like him to taste it and then die, his final act designed to find fault. His apparent death disconcerted me, but I didn't feel sad. The kitchen was like a family and his death was like losing a relative one didn't like. I felt the loss, but not any grief. My lack of compassion made me feel less than human, which increased my churlish mood.

The body stretched behind my compact work area toward where Victor and his second cousin Abundio washed dishes. They were speaking low, rapid-fire Spanish. The only words I picked out were *la chota* and *La Migra*. The death had them worried about the police or immigration showing up.

When the paramedics arrived, I turned to watch, but Abundio slipped out the door to the Vista Dining Room and Victor kept his thick, square back to the excitement. They acted like the INS were imminent. I hadn't thought much before about the routine fear of their lives. No one in the kitchen would rat on them, not even Eldon with his this-is-America-speak-English attitude.

The two paramedics looked like they doubled as lifeguards. "Good job," one said. Todd and Patsy stood, stretched, and rubbed their joints. One of the paramedics hooked Fortier's body to a respirator, and the other exclaimed, "Whoa, I know this dude. He's that famous cook."

No one in the kitchen responded. I glanced at Buzz, but like everyone else, he was acting as if he hadn't heard the paramedic's comment and as if there wasn't a dead body in our midst. He wore the same stoic, stony countenance he'd given me every time I'd prodded and pried about the cooking show.

I looked again at the stiff, quiet workers. Maybe the kitchen crew had convinced themselves the inert mass could be revived. I knew Fortier was dead.

I turned back to the vague shape of Fortier's head pressed into my *lebkuchen*. There was nothing wrong with my dough that could have contributed to his death. It was still cold from its night in a locked refrigerator. We didn't have ingredients for a whole new batch and the specials menu was already printed. I felt a pang of guilt about germs from Fortier, but the oven would destroy them. I shaped the dough into cookies. Then I baked them.

CHAPTER FIVE

Perched atop eighty acres of eucalyptus and redwoods, Archibald's afforded views over Santa Cruz and the Monterey Bay. The elegant, two-story main building, once a Catholic boys' high school, now housed meeting rooms and the restaurant. The police tromped through the main entrance, below an arching facade that cried for the missing cross. They strode through the main lobby, down the hallway to Vista Dining Room and into the kitchen. Eldon was in a dither.

"Good Jesus, what will our customers think?" He wrung his hands as he gave the officers a piece of his mind. Why couldn't they have entered from the loading dock and side entrance like the paramedics?

The two policemen ignored his lecture. They collected names and basic where, what, when information. One left briefly, and not more than twenty minutes later, two detectives in plain clothes arrived. This did not bode well. The appearance of the detectives confirmed the paramedics had been unable to jump start Fortier.

The female detective, a woman of Junoesque proportions, waved to Patsy. Her smock and chef's hat hid her mauve curls, tattoo, and muscle definition. I was surprised an acquaintance would recognize her so easily; she looked normal if one could say that about any of us in our hound's-tooth pants.

Although Eldon had a couple of inches, and many pounds, over the detective, the woman treated him like a gnat, slightly annoying, but hardly a presence with which to reckon. She introduced herself to him as Detective Peters. In spite of her ordinary gray slacks and charcoal blazer, everything about her blared cop.

Her partner was younger and more casual, dressed in Levi's, dress shirt and tie. He had a smooth, kind face, not yet world weary or jaded. A crooked nose added the right touch of toughness. He looked like he'd become a cop out of civic duty or because his father had been one. He didn't look the anal-retentive or power-tripping type. Standing under the mistletoe Fortier had taped to the ceiling only yesterday, he introduced himself to Eldon as Detective Carman and they shook hands.

With pads of paper in their hands, the uniformed officers stood in the middle of the kitchen and read back the information they'd collected to the detectives.

"Buzz?" the female asked.

One of the officers pointed and Buzz turned, holding a small knife. He'd been cutting fresh sage from the kitchen's herb garden. "It's on my driver's license," he said.

When Buzz decided not to talk about something, it was useless to pry, as I'd learned all too well.

The detective seemed to sense this. She glanced warily at the knife and her eyes scanned the room, noting knives everywhere.

The detectives asked the officers a few questions. We all listened, slack-jawed and transfixed, even as we automatically performed our tasks. I stood at the door of the bakery so I could see all the action.

Eldon guided them toward me. "There are three ways into the kitchen from the dock," he said, hinting that the police should use one of them. "There's a door near the walk-in refrigerators, and, if you go through this swinging door into the hallway, there's a door at the end. Off the hallway is the EDR—the Employees' Dining Room—and there's a door out from there as well."

Instead of taking the hint, the detectives assigned one of the uniforms to the dock to watch all the three back exits and another uniform at the passageway between the kitchen and the dining room.

"Isn't that overkill?" Eldon asked. He gulped, as though he immediately regretted his word choice. "I mean is all of this really necessary? People do die from influenza."

The two detectives nodded respectfully, but their eyes were already examining the bakery, down the metal racks, over my body. Eldon bounded off to make sure no one's brunch would suffer just because Fortier had the bad taste to die in the kitchen.

Peters, the female detective, took two long strides to Victor's area, peered into the chute to the abyss of the dishwasher's garbage disposal, inspected Victor and the tray he'd loaded for the conveyor ride through the washer, and touched the swinging straps at the other end. "Looks like a mini-car-wash," she muttered. Peters glanced at the cheap foam cooler under Victor's counter. "What's that for?" Oddly, I'd wondered that a hundred times, but for all my native curiosity, had never asked.

Victor ignored Peters, pulling into himself, his compact body dwarfed by the detective.

She persisted, asking if he'd seen the incident.

"*No entiendo.*" I don't understand.

Her male partner surprised everyone by asking the question in flawless Spanish.

Victor said he hadn't seen anything.

Officer Peters bent down and wiggled off the squeaky top of the cooler. I tried to get a peek over her shoulder. She scowled up at me.

"Is that blood?" she asked Victor.

Her partner translated.

Victor peered into the container and said in Spanish that he didn't know.

I stood on my tiptoes and glimpsed a bit of pinkish liquid in the bottom of the cooler. "We cook meat," I said. "Blood's common in the kitchen."

Since Fortier had not been stabbed or shot, she seemed to lose interest in the blood. "Where's this…" She consulted her notes. "…Abundio?"

Nobody volunteered any information.

Victor replaced the lid of the cooler as Eldon pressed back up behind us. Eldon gave his rendition of events. Detective Peters turned to me. "Fortier collapsed into dough?"

She and Detective Carman both looked over my shoulders

at the five rows of six cookies on each of ten sheets. Detective Carman had the graciousness to breathe in the spicy air, but the female detective widened her eyes.

"Want one?" I asked. "Right out of the oven."

Detective Peters looked at me as though I were a smart ass. "You destroyed evidence?" She had sandy hair, almost as close-cropped as Carman's. I wondered if she had a temper. My mom always associated the highlights in my auburn hair with my temper.

"Evidence of what?"

She didn't want to answer that question. For all my interest in murder, I only then realized Fortier might have been killed. I'd thought the detectives had come because the death was unexpected, what they called "suspicious," on the level of someone having a heart attack and dying at the spa—a death the police investigated, but without much rigor. The thought of actual murder, right where I was standing, lit in my gut and struggled to my brain.

"Were you here when it happened?" Detective Peters asked me.

"The murder?"

She frowned. "No one's used that word."

"No, I wasn't here when it happened. I was over in pastry."

She gave me another one of those looks that said we weren't hitting it off.

She turned back to the main kitchen. She diagrammed the area and snagged Eldon long enough to confirm the names and phone numbers the uniformed cops had gathered. Detective Carman photographed.

"Do you have anyone who saw anything?" Detective Peters asked Eldon, with a hint of weary sarcasm.

"Patsy was over here. She'd brought some bowls for Victor and Abundio to wash." Eldon wrinkled his fleshy forehead, and looked around, his mouth in a moue. Abundio had not returned to the dishwashing station.

Detective Peters walked across the kitchen behind the lead line and back line chefs to the pastry department and returned talking amiably with Patsy. With Patsy's uniform covering her shaved head and tattoos, I was struck by her prettiness. Her widely spaced green eyes were animated by the interaction with the detective. *Was the cop attracted to her?*

"So what was this guy Fortier doing when he collapsed?" Detective Peters switched to business as she and Patsy reached the bakery.

Both detectives kept using that word, as though they didn't even want to say he died until it was official, the relatives contacted, the notice in the paper.

Patsy gestured toward the steps, folded and set aside in the hall. "He was sitting on that stepladder, holding his stomach. He looked like he had the flu." She turned toward the stainless steel table that occupied most of the bakery. "He was sampling Carol's dough."

Both detectives glanced again at the brown, spicy cookies cooling on my counter.

"He didn't die from my *lebkuchen*," I said. I picked up a cookie and bit into it. "Ah shit."

"Are you all right?" Detective Peters asked.

"I forgot the citron."

She snapped on a latex glove and began to bag the cookies.

"You're going to take all of them?" Since, like a king's sampler I'd eaten a mouthful of the cookie without keeling over, I felt the officer was acting out of spite.

She didn't bother to reply.

I shot a look at Eldon hovering near the bakery entrance.

"We already have the specials printed with *lebkuchen* listed," he said plaintively over the detective's shoulder.

"This is evidence," the woman said. "Mr. Fortier ate this stuff. Then died." She shot a suspicious look in my direction. If someone mentioned the conversation in the sports bar, she'd probably cuff me.

"I don't think that's what made Fortier sick," Patsy said. "He was like the expression *green around the gills* before he came to the bakery. I couldn't believe he was eating."

Eating while sick did seem implausible, but why else would he be in the bakery? "Maybe he was so sick that he just sat on the stool to rest." Fortier usually didn't sit in order to sample; he was more the dive-bombing type.

"He had a finger in your dough," Patsy said, as though she thought I'd meant to contradict her—in front of her cohort.

"Ladies," Eldon murmured.

Detective Peters turned toward him with the bags full of warm cookies as though his mild rebuke included her.

"Jean…ehm, that's Mr. Fortier, did say he was sick and going home," Eldon said, trying to gain control. "I asked if he wanted me to call a cab."

I felt claustrophobic with two representatives of the law, plus

Patsy and Eldon boxing me into the nook. I was also anxious about what I could whip up on such short notice to replace the *lebkuchen.*

"So what was he doing here?" Detective Peters asked.

Eldon lifted his big shoulders.

"He could never stay out of the kitchen," I said.

I guess they heard the resentment in my voice. Detective Peters scratched one sandy eyebrow and eyed me speculatively.

"He was always tasting and adding spices and suggesting. He was a pain in the ass," I blurted. It felt refreshing to say that and not worry it'd get back to Jean and my job would be at stake. His near celebrity status had given him more power than the title Head Chef merited.

"You didn't like him?"

"Nobody liked him."

Eldon cleared his throat. "I'm certain this unfortunate incident had nothing to do with my staff. My belief is that Mr. Fortier did leave and returned to drop off his Kris Kringle gift."

"Fortier," I scoffed. "I can't believe he participated."

"He got a present this morning," Eldon said stubbornly. "A jar of honey."

Officer Peters drew a deep breath. "Where is that jar of honey?"

Eldon shook his head. "I haven't seen it since then. Another reason I think he left and returned."

"If he actually left, it's most likely he came back to see Delores," said Patsy.

"That's Delores Medina," Detective Peters said. She sat the evidence bags on my stainless steel table while she checked her notes.

"Right-o."

Patsy led the troop back across the kitchen, turning left before the pastry area, into the garde manger's domain. There the lovely Dorothy Medina worked under the tutelage of the completely different, but equally lovely Suzanne Anderson, turning out salads of bulgar wheat with apricots and dates, mixed greens and spinach, and melons cut into baskets overflowing with crudités.

I could breathe again.

CHAPTER SIX

I caught Chad on the back steps of our tiny house in the banana belt of Santa Cruz. He was smoking a Camel. He started, then quickly stubbed out the cigarette on a potted cyclamen. As much as I adored his James Dean looks, I was adamantly opposed to this detail. Even though the Christmas season told me to be giving, and even though I had exciting news, I unleashed a sarcastic, "That doesn't look or smell like a Vantage."

"It's another type," he said. He stroked Lola, our brindle cat, who rested on a lawn chair. She stretched her front legs and yawned.

"And I know exactly what type." I unpinned my braid and untwisted the ropes of auburn hair.

"Christ, Carol, I spent all morning on a slippery roof in the fog. I need to relax."

"Take a nap." In spite of my tongue, Chad admired the loosened mane. As a kid, I'd hated the wild, thick hair. Now I considered it one of my best features.

"You have no appreciation for how dangerous my job is."

After seeing Fortier dead, less than an hour ago, this remark didn't sit well. "As dangerous as it might be, it's not as dangerous as that thing you had in your mouth. I'm willing to bet more smokers die of cancer than roofers of falls."

He stood and stretched. He was gorgeous. Round buns in 501's, brown, brawny arms exposed by a tee shirt in spite of the December chill. "Well, hello and good afternoon to you." There might have been a wee bit of sarcasm, but basically Chad was easy-going. He meant to change the mood.

"That's it," I said. "If you aren't going to take quitting seriously, I'm buying that life insurance."

I harrumphed through the sliding glass door and stalked into the closet-sized second bedroom of our house. In this sanctuary, I kept my collection of murder mysteries, true crime stories, detective books, and references on guns and poisons. The first three were fine with Chad, but the last spooked him. I'd once hinted that I'd like a gun, just for target practice—there's a gun range up in the hills above Archibald's. Chad had been appalled.

I rifled through hanging file folders for the insurance proposals to prove I was serious about this matter.

Chad leaned in the doorway and watched me silently with blue-green eyes like my own, giving me time to think about how he'd moved his smoking to outdoors, how he'd reduced the quantity, and had switched (for the most part) from Camels to lower tar and nicotine brands. He'd tried Nicorette and even, occasionally, listened to the subliminal messages on the tape I'd bought him.

"I'm trying, Carol."

What more could a person ask? Only a foolish woman would have persisted with a wavy-haired hunk making such an earnest plea. I was she.

"You're only thirty-five and you already have a terrible cough, Chad."

He was gazing sadly at my ringless left hand. If I wore my ring to work, I had a doughy mess at the end of the shift, but Chad didn't seem to understand that. He looked hurt when I forgot to put it back on, as though, without it, I'd be carted off at the end of the day by some womanizer like Fortier.

"How much would you get?" Chad asked.

"A hundred thousand is a standard sort of minimum policy."

He allowed a pregnant pause, and then asked, "Where's that book?" His gaze roamed over my battered desk, and along my bookshelves.

He must have meant my latest acquisition, a reference book that I'd taken to work to browse during break and to shock people. "*Deadly Doses*? That's in my locker, at work, where, incidentally, Jean Alcee Fortier died this morning."

It wasn't the smoothest segue, but now I was ready to change the mood. Then the mournful look in Chad's eyes clicked into place. The poor guy was entertaining the notion that I could have another motive for wanting an insurance policy. The idea struck me as funny and I laughed.

"I don't see anything funny about someone dying." He looked so unsettled that I laughed harder, lost all my annoyance, and tackled him.

"It's not funny," I agreed.

"Then why are you laughing?"

"You..." I managed between hysterical gasps. But, that wasn't it either. The truth was that I may have disliked Fortier, but his death, his possible murder, had twisted me tight all morning and now I was popping loose. All my emotions were spilling out in the form of inappropriate laughter.

Chad appeared stunned as though he thought the maniac sitting on his stomach intended to dispatch him on the spot.

I took a deep breath to still myself and managed to coo, "It'd be much too incriminating to kill you here."

Besides, in spite of my volleyball legs and the arms I'd developed from hefting huge bowls of dough, I couldn't overpower Chad. He remembered that and we wrestled and made up on the Turkish rug. Lola sauntered in to watch this curiosity.

My mood felt significantly improved after we made love on the floor. Chad's defensiveness melted away into my arms. We kissed tenderly, a peace offering as we separated. The phone rang.

"Would you get it?" Chad headed for the bathroom, naked from the waist down.

Half naked, I lifted the receiver. "Hello." I'd never mastered a chirp. I always sounded like someone who hated to answer the phone, which I was.

My greeting wasn't answered. "Hello," I said again. "*Bueno*," I tried in case the person spoke only Spanish. Another thought occurred to me. "Mary? Hello, Mary?"

"Isn't Chad there?"

She hated it when I answered the phone. She was the type of mother who preferred to pretend her son was single.

"He's indisposed."

I could feel her freeze over the phone. "Well, I guess I'll have to take the bus to go shopping," the long-suffering voice began.

"You could call back in five minutes."

"Oh, no, I know he has a busy schedule…"

I zoned out. If she really acknowledged Chad had another life, she wouldn't have called in the first place. I was happy that she wrapped up her self-pity and we said our goodbyes before the toilet flushed.

Chad could deal with the call as he wished. I needed to get going. This was the nineteenth and beyond the little anonymous Kringle gifts I'd already given Esperanza, I'd done no shopping. And now, I also needed to get a sympathy card for Alexis, Fortier's niece who worked second shift.

After taking a shower, I donned fresh jeans and my Jose Cuervo Volleyball Tournament sweatshirt. I hopped into my Karmann Ghia and headed for my favorite shop. I loved my poor man's Porsche even though the exterior was rust red, the interior smelled like dusty oil, and the whole contraption rattled.

Since nearly two hundred people worked at Archibald's, we Kringled within departments and shifts. I had drawn Esperanza's name from Buzz's chef hat. We were surreptitiously to deliver recipes, little gifts, and snacks to our person until Christmas Day. The day after Christmas, when our seasonal push had ended, we'd have our party and exchange the slightly bigger gifts. For now, these were heaped in the upstairs lounge under a fir decorated with red ornaments and tinsel. I felt guilty that I hadn't yet added to the colorful pile, not that Esperanza would care. She wasn't like Suzanne, who shook or poked a package every time she passed the tree.

Tucked behind a health food store, Way of Life featured gallon jars of herbs, natural cosmetic items, a wall devoted to books on herbal, homeopathic, and folk cures, and close, freestanding shelves crammed with gift items. A heady mix of fragrances greeted me at the door.

At the end of one set of shelves, I pawed through a small woven basket of earrings. I tried to imagine some amethyst crystals dangling from Esperanza's ears, but there was something too delicate about them for her. She was a tough lady. Once she'd burned a strip across four fingers that had risen into a path of marble-sized blisters. She'd iced them and finished her shift.

Not that she looked weathered. Her daughter, Delores, had clearly gotten her looks from her mom. They looked more like sisters than mother and daughter. Esperanza was petite, with flawless olive skin, and long, thick black hair just beginning to gray. If the gossip was to be believed, she'd been Fortier's first conquest in the kitchen.

I admired some blown glass vases and turned the corner. My mother-in-law was entering the store. If I'd been in Woolworth's, I wouldn't have been surprised and I would have had an opportunity to evade her.

"Carol," she said, as startled as I was.

To my embarrassment, I realized she was probably shopping for my gift. After years of unworn polyester robes, recycled silk flowers, and unused smelly perfumes, Mary still had no clue what I'd like, but at least she knew more hopeful spots to fish. Thanks, probably, to direction from Chad.

"How'd you get here, Mary?"

"The bus. I can't bother Chad every time I want a ride across town. I know you young folks need time to yourself and I don't want to interfere in your lives." She patted her maroon hair, pursed her red lips, and tugged her tight, nubby yellow jacket over her huge stomach.

She, in fact, called Chad every day. When I mentioned it, Chad cringed and said, "Carol, she's seventy-two." She'd told me that she was sixty-two. His mom lied about everything.

I resented that Mary had never been independent enough to learn to drive or to cut the umbilical cord—unlike my mom, who was also without a husband. My mother had commented years ago, "Carol, why do you always pick men with mothers?"

My conversation with Mary had already ground to an awkward silence. I offered, "I need to find a gift for my Kris Kringle at work."

"Well, honey, I have no idea what young people like."

The tone sounded sympathetic. Yet, I knew she meant we young people, anyone under forty, were difficult and picky.

"You know I'll be working Christmas Eve and Christmas Day," I said, in case she harbored any illusion of a family celebration. I tested the fabric of a small rug between thumb and forefinger.

A customer squeezed around Mary's girth. Mary didn't move. "I don't understand people going out to eat on holidays." She puckered her mouth and in spite of her withered face, managed to look like a baby. "It lacks tradition."

"Brunch or dinner at Archibald's is their tradition."

Another customer entered and detoured to a side aisle. "You

like that rug, honey?"

"Mmmm. Great texture," I said, "but it's light. Slippery." I moved closer to the shelves. "Look at this." I held up a small brass menorah with white candles to lure her from the center of the aisle. Before she could criticize the item, I said, "I'm sure I'll get overtime both days, especially now Fortier is dead."

"The Cruz'n Cuisine King is dead?"

It was no surprise that she knew him. Fortier had become a minor celebrity. And Mary was his ideal audience—stuck at home, an avid television viewer, and a food lover.

I stood in one place, fingering objects, afraid to move with Mary in tow. Besides, of all the aisles, this was the widest. I told her about Fortier's collapse.

"Poisoned," she said with the conviction of a gypsy looking into a crystal ball. "He was poisoned."

CHAPTER SEVEN

The Fortier family managed to arrange a funeral in three days. With Christmas looming, and Fortier's pertinent parts sent to Sacramento for analysis, there was no reason to keep the family in limbo. As busy as Archibald's was, a solid contingent from work attended the service. Even Eldon slid hurriedly into a pew. Officer Peters stood at the back, scanning the chapel full of suspects. She didn't question anyone. Perhaps she was waiting for someone to throw himself over the open coffin and confess.

Officer Peters drew a deep breath and folded her arms. I had the feeling the case didn't interest her much. The paper had given Fortier a nice write-up with the death attributed to an "unknown cause, pending the results from the autopsy." On the day he'd died, the detectives had been called away from Archibald's to a very clear homicide on the West Side. They'd left the uniforms to search for the honey. They did a perfunctory job, like they believed they had a natural death on their hands. They didn't find the jar.

After the service, Suzanne wanted to attend the burial, so I rode with her to Collins Rolling Acres Memorial Park. Fortier was laid to rest where we'd drive by him every day. The graveyard sat across the street from the hospital, providing a cheerful view for patients. The hospital had recently added a residential facility and terminally ill customers could travel in a convenient circuit from hospital to housing to grave, a route my brother Donald could have used.

I liked Collins Rolling Acres. The cemetery lacked the manicured green of places like Forest Lawns, suburbia for dead people. Here, after five years of water conservation, only hardy grass survived. Even in fifty-degree December chill, the place had charm. The markers dated back a hundred years, old enough to be historically interesting, yet none of them was ostentatious or pretentious. I wished Donald had chosen a plot here so that I'd have a solid place to mourn him.

The priest intoned the lovely "earth to earth, ashes to ashes, dust to dust, in sure and certain hope of the resurrection onto eternal life." As Fortier's casket was lowered into the raw new hole, my heart ached for my brother, his ashes floating, or dissolved, in the salty sea out from Ft. Bragg. My poor mom, the victim of a cosmic mix-up. First she'd had Donald; then she'd had me. Since Donald didn't "come out" until his twenties, I had a huge head start on giving her grief. To hear my mom, I first refused to get born, but when I finally plopped on to the delivery table, I asked for cowboy boots and a gun. God had definitely gotten her orders scrambled. I'd once heard someone ask my mom about grandchildren, to whom she'd dryly responded, "My children don't reproduce."

Those who wanted stepped forward to toss clods of earth onto the casket. I liked the hollow thud, the note of finality. The reminder of our fragile, precarious state filled me with needed humility. I wished Donald had chosen this ceremony instead of cremation.

As we dispersed from the pit, Suzanne fell in step beside me. She dabbed at the corner of an eye.

I gave her a brief, sideways hug. "You okay?"

"He had his good points," she snuffled. Dressed in black stirrup stretch pants and a mid-thigh black cashmere sweater, she looked pale and lovely.

"Of course."

She looked at me suspiciously, although I'd meant to concede the point. I'd never met a pure swine or angel. People were complicated. I had only to look at my small family. On one hand, while Donald had promiscuously used sex to make a point, my mother referred to him as a "bachelor," even as he was dying of AIDS.

"Hey," Suzanne said, "your eyes are teary."

I nodded in acknowledgment.

Suzanne's brown eyes peered into my damp ones. "Hey," she said, "did you…did Jean…?"

"Oh, no." I stuck out my puny chest. "Me? Now if Fortier had been a leg man…. Nah, he only liked me for my scintillating personality."

She sighed and her body relaxed. "Jean was generous, fun to be with, and great in bed."

"I'm sure he was." I hoped my tone sounded comforting. Given Fortier's success with women, I'd assumed the latter. I also had no trouble believing that when he took out a woman, he wined her and dined her in a slow-paced luxury that blinded her to the inevitable conclusion.

I tried to imagine Suzanne crazed with jealousy, concocting a poisonous brew to kill Fortier. But even aided by Suzanne's black clothes and somber mood, I couldn't imagine her as a murderess. In theory, I believed everyone capable of murder. I certainly was. Yet, I told myself that if Suzanne had killed Fortier, it would have been an accident. I realized fully that I believed Fortier had been murdered, that Mary was right about the method, and that I was damned interested in finding out who done it. I wanted to untangle the puzzle, but more than that, I wanted to know if one of my friends could have committed the crime.

"Who was that with Alexis?" Suzanne asked.

I looked up the knoll to see if I could spot Fortier's diminutive niece, although I knew to whom Suzanne was referring. I was surprised she had not already gotten the scoop on Alexis's companion. Suzanne was losing her touch. "That's Fortier's ex."

"I didn't know he'd been married."

"Me neither."

Suzanne's yellow bug was parked in a lane that curved around the low hill. Suzanne perched on the wheel well of her car and diddled with the black ruffle in her hair.

"Good thing we both have skinny butts," I said, bumping her to create room for me. Behind us, near the groundskeeper's house, the lines of the flagpole dinged in the crisp air. I glanced toward the wooded hills leading to Archibald's while Suzanne lit a clove cigarette.

She exhaled pungent smoke. "So how did you find out about Fortier's ex?"

Other mourners trickled down to their cars. Alexis and the mystery woman left the grave with a man who had to be Fortier's brother—Alexis' father—and the tiny, white-haired mom, her old face red with silent weeping.

"Eldon. He called Alexis when Fortier died." I didn't feel ready to share my suspicions. "This woman answered and said she was Julieanne Fortier. When Eldon heard the name, he asked who she was."

"She's not what I'd expect," Suzanne whispered as the four black figures approached. In deference, she ground the cigarette against the tire, put the unsmoked portion in a small enameled case, and tucked it into her black clutch bag.

"Except for the tits, me either," I whispered back. The inside of Fortier's locker at work left no doubt about his predilections. Julieanne was plain with shoulder length, brown curled hair. Her body was not fat, but lacked muscle tone. From years of observing naked women at the Spa, I knew how she'd look undressed, her stomach, butt and thighs dimpled with cellulite, her breasts losing the fight against gravity, not a match I would have imagined for Fortier.

"What was she doing in Santa Cruz?" Suzanne asked.

I sprang up from the wheel well. "That's what I plan to find out."

CHAPTER EIGHT

When I opened the door, Chad was wrapping a large box in red foil. He labored in the middle of the oak floor.

"For me?" I asked coyly, putting hands over my eyes. Through the peek holes, I spotted his mom at the end of the couch, planted like a Buddha. I grimaced at her, all playfulness vanishing. I disliked this woman from the maroon hair down to the duck feet crammed into shoes that she pretended fit because they'd been on sale. In a week, she'd want Chad to haul her to the podiatrist. Compared to the roiling I felt in Mary's presence, my past reactions to Fortier seemed like sardonic amusement.

"Hello, Carol," Mary said in a voice that might fool Chad as he wasn't looking at her. The small eyes pinned me with loathsome jealousy that declared I'd never fully appreciate this gift. "We couldn't find any scissors for the paper."

No, *"How was the funeral?"*

"You couldn't find the scissors, Chad?" I wasn't having any of her "we" shit. At her house scissors would have been easily located, not because she was organized, but because she had four or five pairs.

Chad shrugged. "No problem. I just tore it. You're gonna love this present, Carol." He beamed.

"Don't tell me what it is." I departed to our bedroom. I couldn't watch Chad wrap. We wrapped to different drummers. Plus Chad would start dropping hints, while I liked surprises. I'd have to work to keep this present a secret, even with only two measly days until Christmas. I also wanted to get away from Mary and change out of my black skirt and heels into some sweat pants.

On the nightstand I kept my one photo of Donald, his senior picture. I picked up the heavy, pewter frame. He looked clean-cut, handsome, athletic and straight, as he no doubt yearned to be. What could be more painful than being a homosexual teenager? I turned the plastic latches on the back, popped out the cardboard, and removed the paper from behind the photograph. I'd cut it from the program for his service. One thing about dying slowly, you could plan your funeral. Donald had chosen this passage from Lewis Thomas' *The Lives of a Cell*: "The obituary pages tell us of the news that we are dying away while the birth announcements in finer print, off at the side of the page, inform us of our replacements, but we get no grasp from this of the enormity of the scale. There are 3 billion of us on the earth and all 3 billion must be dead, on a schedule, within this lifetime. The vast mortality, involving something over 50 million of us each year, takes place in relative secrecy…."

I guess that put death in perspective, I thought, as I returned the clipping to its spot, but it made me feel so gloomy that I returned to the living room. Chad was putting the Scotch tape into a kitchen drawer.

"I got a great deal," Chad said. He held the package (about as big as a bread box) against his plaid flannel shirt. Tape bandaged the bright red.

Chad's mention of a "deal" filled me with apprehension. Possibly this was the beginning of his evolution into a person like Mary, a person whose life was ruled by the word "sale." Although Mary lived on Social Security, I'd known her to buy ten chickens at Safeway because they were on sale. Of course, she'd had nowhere to freeze them, so that had meant an instant party. Barbecue was the easiest, but she didn't have a grill. But we did. I feared Chad would become Mary, just as I feared that I'd fall into my mother's world of cliché. Even hating my mother-in-law seemed like cliché.

"Wanna feel how heavy it is?" Chad asked.

"Nah, that's okay, Chad." I didn't need to touch it to guess he'd bought a CD player. We'd discussed the idea several times.

He lowered the gift to beside our potted tree that we'd hauled in from the back yard. The box dwarfed it.

"I feel bad, Chad. I don't even have an idea for your present. Unless you want a plot at Collins Rolling Acres Memorial Park. At the funeral, I thought it would be a nice place to be buried."

Mary fanned herself with a scrap of wrapping paper. "Thinking about such stuff at your age isn't natural. Now, when you are old and decrepit like me, that's a different story."

My hatred of Mary was unfair as she couldn't focus on me long enough to hate me back with the same intensity.

"When I was your age...." She stopped, trying to remember either what my age was, or what she was doing back then.

Normally, Chad would have started a peace-keeping campaign by now. Instead he wrinkled his forehead. "Boy that funeral put you in a cheery mood."

I forgave his sarcasm. If I'd spent the afternoon with his mom, I'd be way beyond cutting remarks. He was probably miffed, too, that I hadn't paid proper attention to his gift.

His mother smiled, happy at the hint of dissension. The simper didn't even unwrinkle her lips.

"Mary said Fortier was poisoned." His inflection seemed to add, *And where is that poison book of yours*? This was silly. Was Chad entertaining the idea of me as the killer?

"Geez, Chad, I'm not going to slip hemlock into your eggnog." I peered in the refrigerator for a snack. "At least, not until you're fully insured." I pivoted and watched with satisfaction as Mary's lips dried into prunes. The down side was the small jolt, like a muscle spasm, in Chad's neck.

"Do the police have any suspects in the Cuisine King's murder?" The timing of her question and her emphasis on the last word dripped with implication. She sniffed, her lips puckered. Her eyes squinted into boreholes.

"Detective Peters attended the service," I said, "but they haven't even declared Fortier's death a homicide."

"Channel 8 called it a suspicious death," Chad said. He was sweeping up scraps of paper and ribbon.

I felt piqued that I'd missed the television coverage. Eldon had done a great job of suppressing the news. The *Sentinel* article had been second-page and more focused on Fortier's career than his sudden death.

"Let me do that, honey." Mary struggled from the couch, making an elaborate show of reaching for the broom, in spite of her poor, swollen feet.

"Sit down, Mary." Chad called his mom by name because she had abandoned him to her parents on a dairy farm near Ferndale, while she'd drifted around the country, trying to make a living, experimenting with various partners and lifestyles. His grandmother was mom.

"You need some help, son."

"I don't need any help."

"This murder is just the gruesome thing to interest Carol." Mary settled her large rump back onto the cushions.

My neck prickled with antagonism. "I do think it's more stimulating than a sale at Mervyn's."

Mary's thin eyebrows shot up, but she wore a tight smile.

Chad sighed as he emptied the dustpan.

"You better watch out that Carol doesn't start playing detective," Mary said.

"Hello, Mary." I pranced in front of her, crossing my arms like semaphores. "Yo, over here." I was regressing quickly, and I hated her for it. "I am in the room."

"Well, I know you are, dear." Her saccharine voice was smug with victory. She'd reduced me to a twelve-year-old right before my husband's eyes. "I'm telling my son this because I don't think he knows."

"Knows what?"

She blinked her stubby, painted lashes like it should be obvious what she meant. That was the flash point. I burned to my scalp. Chad didn't need to worry that I might investigate a murder; he needed to worry that I'd commit one. "If I decided to play detective," I spit into the wrinkled face, "I'd be damned good at it."

She smiled with condescending patience, secure in the protection of her son.

Chad decided to whisk Mary away from his half-crazed wife, across town to her one-bedroom HUD apartment near the railroad tracks. They roared off in his Ford truck and my bad mood left with them.

When the mail came, Lola followed me out to the old-fashioned metal box on a post. "Let's see if you won that cat food sweepstakes."

She meowed in agreement and looked up.

Inside the box were some junk mail fliers and a letter from a screenwriter, a distant friend. I'd written him in a flurry of excitement about an idea for a movie: a woman collects a cool million in insurance money after she knocks off her drunken husband by plastering his chest with nicotine patches. My distant friend politely thanked me, and then asked a barrage of questions about the story that indicated he found the plot implausible.

"Have you ever thought you might be in the wrong line of work?" he'd written. "I can't imagine you braiding dough. You should be a private investigator, a reporter on the city desk, or maybe a mortician."

As I walked to the house, I hugged the European-style writing paper to my heart. Someone who believed in me!

Lola protested: "Open the door, my pompous, silly person." She meowed indignantly. "I thought I'd trained you better than this."

I opened the door and made a resolution. I'd bury Chad's mom without killing her. She'd rue the day she'd made that quip about my being a detective.

CHAPTER NINE

The next day after work, I sat glumly at the indoor fountain at the Capitola Mall. The water had been turned off and the circle converted to a Christmas wonderland. I detested the mall, especially the day before Christmas. The hordes. The masses. The mind-numbing joviality. My chest tightened, the way it had many moons ago at rock concerts, but now it wasn't from eau de marijuana. What if something excited the crowd? A fire? An earthquake? A blue light special? A person could be trampled.

The mall reminded me of the plant in *Little Shop of Horrors*. It fed on people and grew and grew. The growth had exceeded the ability of the lifelines to support it. Coming from the south at this busy time, one waited through four or five changes of the light to exit the freeway to 41st Avenue. Then the traffic moved like blood through a clogged artery.

I looked around for local television crews who roamed malls on Christmas Eve to humiliate last minute shoppers.

I'd considered buying Chad a CD case containing several choice discs, maybe even a best of Van Halen strictly for him. To go with the CD player. But Chad didn't know how obvious he was and I didn't want to enlighten him.

I also needed something for my mom. Her gift to me would be crocheted, possibly useful, but just as likely to be an orange toaster cover.

Questions about what to buy Chad and how to investigate Fortier's murder bumped and mixed in my head with piped-in Christmas carols and the tidal hum of hundreds of frantic shoppers. I sat at the edge of the waterless fountain and dug my hand into a box of caramel popcorn. I liked snacks that I could grind between my teeth and that I didn't see at Archibald's.

The police were investigating Fortier's suspicious death, but the tox screen would be done in Sacramento. It could take weeks before they officially declared the death a homicide.

The kitchen staff seemed determined to believe that Fortier had been gripped by a massive coronary. But, for once in my life, I agreed with Mary. The quick, deadly flu-like symptoms Eldon reported suggested poison. I couldn't understand how someone like Mary, who had the sensitivity of a whetstone, could have figured that out. Yesterday when Chad had returned from taking her home, he'd said worriedly, "Mary thinks you're going to get tangled up in this."

"I'd make a good detective," I'd grumbled, rankled that my distant friend, the screenwriter, could recognize that, but Chad couldn't.

"That may be so, but you're not a detective."

He was right, but I felt like he was siding with Mary. "I could be like Rat Dog."

"Rat Dog?"

"Don't worry. She doesn't have a gun. She just tracks down dirty rats."

"She's real?"

"Shit yeah," I'd said, pissed off by Mary's phony concern, that now had Chad worried. Without a doubt, the woman intended to undermine me, but she was so disorganized and inconsistent with her attacks, I could never formulate an effective defense.

Even now, after cooling off for twenty-four hours, I felt irritated as I replayed the scene. I bit into an "old maid" kernel, shooting pain up my jaw and temple. I tried discreetly to pick the ground seed from a molar, but with my short nails, I had to abandon delicacy. Naturally, that was when I spotted the blond reporter in her tailored suit, wielding her mike and leading a man with a video camera. Fortunately, they missed my excavation and honed in on a big, frantic-looking man in the corridor. My head swiveled back to the man.

Eldon.

He was the last person I wanted to see, but I wondered what inspired him to frenzied shopping. I decided to tail him. He ducked into a jewelry store, as though evading the press. For a simple evasion, Eldon was going to extremes. He confronted a weary-looking clerk, and began such a self-absorbed monologue that I entered the store behind him with no fear of detection. The slender clerk, who looked as though he'd rather be anywhere else, set a velvet tray on the glass counter.

"Yes, something along these lines," Eldon said. "She has brown eyes, so I think gold findings would look better than silver, don't you?" The young man opened his mouth, but Eldon continued. "Delicate, not clunky."

The clerk lifted a pair.

"More feminine."

The clerk glanced past Eldon at me, so I edged out the open entrance and melted into the flow headed toward Sears.

To me, everyone in the kitchen was now a suspect, so I considered Eldon for a moment. He was the fussy, methodical kind who might use a poison, but why would he knock off Fortier, who'd added prestige to his kitchen?

Poison was a rare way to kill. According to my books, it accounted for about one half of one percent of homicides. However, poison was also a smart way to kill, and I imagined people got away with it, which skewed the statistics. What I couldn't understand was why anyone, poisoned and sick, would stop in the bakery to eat *lebkuchen* dough.

Sears' furniture section spread to my right. I plopped into a cozy, tweedy armchair and tried to imagine Eldon with a woman, someone for whom he'd buy earrings. From the chair's safety, I gazed at the shoppers in the stunned state that malls induce in me.

In the past, when I'd wanted to know more about crime, I had pestered both the coroner and Sergeant Gold of Homicide. Both had tolerated me on the phone, probably because they didn't know how to hang up on a woman. I'd never met either man. For all I knew, they could be among the frenetic shoppers.

To investigate, I'd have to question everyone from the morning kitchen shift. That task would be formidable even if people cooperated, and even if I didn't count the wait staff who moved between the kitchen and dining rooms; Big Red, the cook in the employees' dining room; or the housekeeping staff who picked up dirty towels and uniforms and delivered fresh ones.

Besides, for all the excellent motivations in the kitchen, weren't these things usually domestic? And, poison seemed like a woman's method. Of course, that same reasoning could point to his lovers in the kitchen. He'd worked his way through the women as though searching for an answer by process of elimination—Esperanza, Suzanne, Delores and God knew who else. I had to start somewhere, and even though she wasn't employed in the kitchen, the ex-wife seemed as good a place as any.

No time like the present, even if it were a cliché, Christmas Eve, and the day after the funeral.

Alexis probably had not only Fortier's ex-wife Julieanne, but also her father and grandmother staying with her. With an effort, I lifted myself from my warm nest. The swarm had thinned, but I dodged the remaining desperate shoppers, who hurtled from store to store like juggernauts. At the entrance of the shopping center, I called Alexis at Archibald's. She couldn't see me that night, or on Christmas, but she still planned to go to our employees' party the day after, and promised to talk to me then.

I escaped the mall, drove across the street to a record store, purchased a handsome oak CD holder and several discs—Springsteen, Hungarian Rhapsodies, Garth Brooks, and Poi Dog Pondering. I'd wrap each CD separately, disguising the shapes to create suspense. I meandered down to the Capitola Book Cafe and bought my mom a book. I could wrap at leisure, as Chad had taken his mom to Mass and would dine at her apartment.

Now that I'd solved my shopping problems, I had only a murder case to solve.

CHAPTER TEN

Working on Christmas Day was brutal, not because I was sentimental or minded being at work on the holiday, but because I had to crank out fourteen hundred pieces—stars and apple strudel and cranberry Danish pockets from puff pastry; Danishes with raspberry jelly and jalapeño jelly, and sugar cookies in Christmas shapes.

As I twisted dough, I sifted through the usual motives for murder—love, money and revenge. Revenge suggested Buzz. Love? That got messy fast. Money? I had trouble grasping money as a motive. It didn't seem like there could ever be enough. Not for murder.

I hated raw dough, but I pulled a little piece from my finger and nibbled it, trying to remember if I'd put in the vanilla. Normally I liked my day to be busy. "Idle hands make the devil's playground," had been instilled in me from youth, but today my mind wandered farther afield than automatic pilot. The nibble made me suspicious.

"Carol, want to see me walk on my hands?" Victor asked. He was Esperanza's brother and Delores's uncle, but had a whole other set of genes. His flat, indigenous face more striking than handsome, he grinned at me from the door.

I pinched a marble of dough and thrust it at his face.

"First taste this."

It was a routine command, and he ate from my finger with closed eyes and exaggerated smacking. "Tase like…," he smacked some more, "...tase like dough. Gringo food. No tase."

"Does it need salt?"

He pinched another sample from the mound on my table and repeated the charade. "No."

"All right. Let me see you walk on your hands."

He made a show of wiping his hands on one of my white towels as though preparing for a cartwheel. He stooped and placed his foot on one hand, then the other.

I smiled.

"Good joke, huh?"

"Great joke."

He turned to go. Tasting and joking were the depth of our relationship.

"Victor, how much money would it take for you to kill someone?"

He straightened to his full height, which was about five eight because his offended eyes stared right into mine. "Me kill someone?"

"A hypothetical situation," I said. "Pretend."

"If I don' like the *cabron*, if he raped my sister or something, I do it for free," he said. "But I wouldun' kill someone I like." He scratched his dark hair. "Not for a million dollars." In Spanish he bade me a good day and spun on his heels.

Well, Victor felt as I did, but I knew that people did kill for money, sometimes piddly sums if they were desperate. With his recent successes, Fortier could have a nice nest egg. One person might know about Fortier's financial affairs, but it wasn't going to be easy to extract any information from Concepción Galisanao.

Not even a former Employee of the Year escaped Christmas duty, but then Concepción rivaled Eldon for company loyalty and probably would have been at work even if she could have stayed home. Down the hall in personnel, the tiny woman had been at Archibald's since its opening, which given the hospitality business's turnover, made her an institution. Concepción was the Head of Human Resources. She sat primly at her desk, reading over half glasses. She'd adored Fortier, not because she was fooled, but because she felt it was nice that he bothered to flirt with someone her age.

I extended two cellophane-wrapped brownies.

"Oh, Carol, my favorite!" She smiled up at me, wagging a finger back and forth in the air, the nail manicured and painted with a minuscule wreath. "But no time off."

I held onto the brownies. A person would never surmise from the woman's figure that Concepción lived on a candy bar diet—one delicious Hershey's for breakfast, another for lunch, and a wholesome, satisfying Symphony bar for dinner.

She fanned herself with the papers she'd been considering. "Too hot for Christmas," she said in her accented, helpless voice that made people forget that she was ruthlessly competent.

I wondered if the ageless Concepción Galisanao could be having a hot flash. Her office felt cool to me. But then, I'd been in the bakery all morning. Any place would seem cool to me. I sat opposite her. She wore a red dress; candy cane earrings peeped from her dark hair. From this distance, she could smell the brownies, made with pieces of Belgium chocolate. I played with the cellophane to make sure.

"No time off for anyone until we hire someone." She smiled. "No time off forever." A ring-bedecked hand with a Christmas decoration painted on each nail crept toward the brownies.

"Fortier's death was tragic." I lifted the brownies from the desk.

She gave me a tight smile and one, slow blink of her eyes. "Tragic? You didn't kill him?"

Concepción was impervious to bullshit, which was why everyone liked her.

"So you think he was murdered?"

She shrugged. "That's for the police to decide." The sibilance slurred with saliva. She smiled. Concepción Galisanao could smile as she scheduled you for sixty hours. "Maybe you say it's tragic because no time off."

"No, I think it's tragic because someone killed him. I want to know who."

"One of the women in the kitchen," Concepción declared.

"Maybe. I intend to find out."

Her chocoholic's eyes, transfixed on the two brownies, misted.

"I heard Fortier got a big raise after his program took off."

"Everybody heard that."

"Well?"

"Ten thousand dollars."

"Whew!"

"Not really whew when you consider our wages," Concepción said.

"How about the beneficiary of his insurance policy, Concepción?"

"I can't do that."

I peeled the cellophane from a brownie. "I know. Employee confidentiality. But Fortier's dead."

"Are you going to eat that damned thing?" Concepción snapped.

"I brought them for you."

"Then let me have them, Carol." The little woman lunged for the brownies.

I jerked them away. "Careful, Concepción," I said, "you're going to smush them, and these are ultra fudge masterpieces with hunks of walnut. Crispy outside and chewy centers."

Concepción crossed her arms. "I can get some from the kitchen."

I smiled smugly. "No, you can't."

Concepción walked to a file cabinet and found the hanging folder. "Jean upped the standard work policy to twenty thousand and the beneficiary is...." She turned to me with her nose wrinkled, "His wife?"

"Ex-wife," I corrected.

"Says 'wife.'"

I looked over her shoulder. Under beneficiary it said in Fortier's scribble: Julieanne Fortier—wife. He was a bigger sleaze than I'd thought—not just dating the daughter of a former flame, but dating both while married.

I handed Concepción the brownies. “Thanks. You’ve been a big help.”

CHAPTER ELEVEN

Christmas night was not a success. I did my best to act surprised as I ripped open my big present from Chad, but I'd never been a gifted actress. My lack of oohs and ahs translated in Chad's mind as disappointment. Plus, Christmas reminded him that I didn't attend church, that I was, as his mother put it, "a heathen." Chad fell into a melancholy funk.

Now as I padded over the mauve carpet of Archibald's lobby, through murmurs of my colleagues' conversation, I hoped this day-after-Christmas party proved more fun. I looked forward to buttonholing people to find out more about Fortier. Fortier's niece Alexis didn't have any buttonholes in her black velvet frock. I seized her tiny wrist and towed her to the balcony. She didn't know me that well, but she didn't protest.

"Whadzup?" she asked in typical twenty-something banter. Her nearly black eyes looked annoyed, but curious.

Out on the balcony, the fog swirled up the hill, obscuring any view and dampening our faces. At last year's party, several drunken employees had leapt from the balcony to the lawn below. One of the cooks, Big Red, had broken his leg. This year the party was *sans* alcohol and subdued. There'd been other such changes in the last year. After a series of prime rib and steak thefts, Eldon had installed padlocks on the walk-in refrigerators.

I hadn't thrown on my coat and the chill penetrated my long-sleeved, turtleneck dress. "I'm sorry about your uncle," I said.

"Yeah, right." The fog diffused Alexis's petite frame but I heard the spite.

"He was an excellent chef and my heart goes out to you."

"You guys all hated him!" The apparition flounced by to the rail. "Probably one of you killed him. Like that bitch Patsy!"

I followed cautiously, as though sneaking up on a tiny, flitting finch. "Patsy?" I prompted.

"You know how some women are when they can't get what they want."

I nearly laughed. Patsy want Fortier? But maybe she knew something I didn't. At least she wasn't in denial about the murder like the rest of the kitchen.

I hadn't known what to expect. I saw Alexis only occasionally when I ate in the EDR after my shift and she came in early to take advantage of the free food.

As I leaned on the balcony rail, she jumped away from me. Alexis looked like Fortier but the strong Gallic features were less dashing on a young woman. "He was eating your batter!"

Dough, I mentally corrected. "Yeah, I don't understand that part," I said, "but I agree he was killed."

Her eyes grew to the size of quarters. "I can understand why you guys didn't like him." Those wide eyes were now shiny with tears. "But as an uncle, he was great. Generous. He got me this job, you know?"

"I know." She was the second person to mention Fortier's generosity. He'd lived in a condo near the yacht harbor that was worth at least a hundred thousand. He'd received money from Exploration's acquisition of the cooking program and from a hefty raise. Plus he had a cookbook in the works. Now he was dead, would his wife Julieanne profit from his generosity? At the funeral, she'd looked a little down in the heel.

"I'm surprised you had Jean's ex-wife come stay with you," I said.

"Julieanne? I don't think they divorced." She didn't sound sure. "Besides, she's my godmother. Jean was my godfather. Neither of them had any kids, and they competed for me. Especially after my mom left." She sighed. "I liked the attention and money and stuff, but it was kind of exhausting."

"Are your dad and grandmother still here?"

"No. Julieanne drove them to the airport so I could come to the party." She sounded worried. "I should have done it."

"Why?"

She chose not to answer.

"If Jean and Julieanne are separated, what brought her to Santa Cruz?" I tried to sound nonchalant, while rubbing the goose bumps on my arms. I pulled down the sleeves that I would push up in another minute, a habit from years of working in dough.

"I like to think she came here because of me," Alexis said. She pulled a tissue from the pocket of the velvet cape she'd thrown over her dress. "But she came here because of Jean. They split up fifteen years ago, and she's still not over him." She delicately blew her nose. "I guess she'll have to get over him now."

From her tone, I realized that Julieanne had been in town for a while. "What did she do in Santa Cruz?"

Alexis's eyes narrowed. "Why are you asking me all this stuff?"

"Because I think the same thing you do. I think Jean was murdered."

"So why do you give a shit?" Her eyes flicked over me. "Were you one of his girlfriends?"

I shook my head. "Not his type." The fact made me feel pissed off at Fortier even though he was dead. Because I clearly wasn't his type, I couldn't mistake his harassment for anything else.

In spite of her hostility, Alexis didn't walk off. She wanted to talk. I stared into the mist, waiting.

"Julieanne worked at KRUZ-TV as an office manager."

I felt like saying something dumb like, "Holy cow," or "No kidding?" No wonder Alexis acted as if she were making a confession. The information held all kinds of implications. I didn't want to ask my next question. I felt as though I'd already taken advantage of Alexis's vulnerability.

I was lucky; I didn't have to. Alexis volunteered the information. "I'm sure she helped Jean steal Buzz's show."

CHAPTER TWELVE

Alexis had assumed the morning crew's silence regarding Fortier's theft of the show was due to ignorance rather than discretion. Tact, like rumaki and caviar canapés, is a taste developed with age. She told me what I already knew, that Buzz had planned the Cruz'n Cuisine show. "Everything, even the title, was his idea."

She whirled around. "I'm too cold out here." I followed as she pushed through one set of French doors into the heart of the party.

Tables of hors d'oeuvres had been set up opposite the Christmas tree. Boiled shrimp piled on a bowl of ice, garnished with lemons. Frittatas baked in pie dishes sat on one side, and an array of crudité and dips on the other. I wondered if I'd have a chance to eat, as I planned to do some serious mingling. People milled, crowded the plush mauve chairs and couches, and nibbled shrimp with mango sauce between sips of sparkling apple juice. I wistfully eyed their plates.

"So how'd Julieanne get KRUZ to switch to your uncle?" I asked Alexis.

Eldon, dressed as Santa Claus, stood behind a food table spread with desserts. As we passed, he handed each of us a paper plate with a petit four. "The pink one's for Alexis," he said. "My own creations."

Alexis led me away from the crowd into the wide hallway to Vista Dining Room. A few people sprinkled the hallway, admiring the art display, recorded by discreet cameras installed to discourage theft. Alexis glanced at my plate. "I'd rather have chocolate frosting."

"Here. I'll trade with you." Her petit four was topped with a sugary rose. I didn't care which cake I had since my work had numbed my appetite for sweets.

"Julieanne kept Jean posted on Buzz's progress," Alexis said softly. She nibbled a bit of cake with her front teeth like a rabbit. "Buzz made his pitch and the producer liked the idea. That's when…"

Alexis froze. Then she abruptly turned to the wall as though enraptured by the watercolors on display. Walking towards us from Vista Dining Room were Suzanne Anderson and Buzz Fraser.

Suzanne looked cold in an electric blue dress that scalloped over her breasts and ended well before the knees. The tiny bolero jacket looked like scant comfort. She walked arm in arm with Buzz, but I doubted they had a date. Suzanne liked to flirt, and Buzz was an accommodating guy. Probably she was snuggling against him to keep warm.

"Hi, guys," I hailed them.

Alexis whirled toward me, her face red, her dark eyes resentful.

"I have to go to the restroom." She clipped back toward the lounge as fast as her spike heels would allow.

"What's eating Alexis?" Suzanne asked. She removed the blue band from her hair and slipped the elasticized ruffles around her wrist.

I shook my head, although I had an idea.

Buzz Fraser watched the long, dark hair billowing behind Alexis. The young woman slowed only to toss her unfinished petit four in the garbage. I tried to read Buzz's expression, but he was noted for his unflappable nature in a work place where people had monumental egos. His look might have been one of concern or mere curiosity, but he did watch her until she disappeared into the restroom. Then he gave me a hug. Buzz wore soft brown cords and a warm, woolen sweater in a swirl of mellow earth tones. Even in the brief embrace, he felt warm. He smelled like eggnog, although I hadn't seen any at the party.

"Where's Chad?" he asked.

"He refused to be dragged. Spouses need alcohol to make these things bearable."

This wasn't true. Chad liked to talk to people, but given my intention to snoop, I hadn't encouraged him to come. He'd been a little hurt and suspicious.

"Are you just going to admire that cake?" Suzanne asked.

I held the poinsettia-designed paper plate aloft and cast a critical eye on the petit four's rose. "Why not? It's Eldon's *objet d' art*."

Suzanne frowned. "Eldon might say that, but the flower is pure Patsy."

"Since Chad isn't here, I'll expect you to dance with me," Buzz said.

"You bet."

A force of personality, polar to Fortier's, rendered Buzz so attractive. He possessed an unpretentious calm.

I wanted to do more than dance with Buzz Fraser.

CHAPTER THIRTEEN

Back in the lounge, the tall Santa Claus fumbled a tiny green package. Buzz got us each a coffee, and I perched on the arm of a couch, with my elbow on his shoulder. Suzanne leaned on the back of Abundio's chair. The young dishwasher looked back at her, blushed, and squirmed with pleasure. Other employees sat haphazardly on the windowsills, couches, and thick carpet.

"This is Christmasy," Buzz whispered, touching the ends of my scarf.

I'd tied it around my shoulders at the last minute for the Christmas colors in the pattern of bright red roses and green leaves on a gold background. It was like Buzz to notice exactly what a person wanted noticed.

My loose hair spread down over my shoulders and Buzz touched it, the way a person might sample a fabric between fingers.

I set aside my paper cup of coffee. It was a blend with a hazelnut flavor, but I liked coffee black and unadulterated. A bit of a purist. I sampled the pink flower with my finger. It was pure. Pure sugar. I didn't want to abandon it where Eldon might see it since he'd claimed it was his special creation.

As Santa, Eldon was in his element—center stage, in-charge, promoting the company. He was a born bureaucrat and must have been miserable as a cook, before he worked his way up to head of the kitchen.

He called for the fourth time, "Alexis?"

People didn't bother to look around. They wanted Eldon to get on with it. He reluctantly returned the package to the still large pile below the tree.

Buzz didn't ask what had happened to Alexis. Buzz, ever the perceptive one, must have noticed his effect on her.

Eldon picked up a red foil box, all tape hidden, a lavish white bow on top. While I'd never buy a dress or shoes with bows, they looked good on presents.

"This is for Esperanza." Eldon leaned back and made a ho, ho, ho.

I bent down and whispered in Buzz's ear. "Let's sneak out to the balcony."

"Don't you want to see what Esperanza got?" he teased.

"Glow in the dark Band-Aids, aloe vera cream for burns, and a spatula so she can quit borrowing mine."

He arched one pale eyebrow.

"I have a black sense of humor." I picked up the petit four thinking to dispose of it somewhere out of Eldon's sight.

Buzz smiled, a rare phenomenon that transformed the severe Scottish features. "I don't know. That's what Esperanza would like."

There he went again. Saying exactly what I wanted. Reassuring.

"She's a pretty earthy lady," he added. He held the door for me as others noted our escape. "Even if she did have that thing with Fortier."

Cold fog enveloped us. Buzz hugged me sideways into the warmth of his sweater and I almost dropped the petit four. We walked to the rail and peered into the nothingness.

"When did they have their fling, anyway? It was before my time."

"Except for me, Fortier and Esperanza, it was before everybody's time."

"Before Eldon's?"

"Oh, yeah. Fifteen years ago, at least. I have to give Esperanza credit, though. She's the only lady I know who ever dumped him."

This was news to me. "What happened?"

"If I remember right, she had a husband who suddenly resurfaced—or something like that."

"You know, don't you, that I think Fortier was murdered?"

"Yeah," he whispered, as though we were having a romantic conversation. "This thing Fortier had going with Delores is more complicated than people think."

"How so?"

"Esperanza broke his heart. I think he was in love with her."

"So Delores was a revenge?"

He shrugged and spread wide the fingers of his free hand. "Maybe it was a silly attempt to recapture the love."

My baker's nose again detected eggnog. With rum. "I want to figure out who killed him."

"Be careful, Carol. Nobody likes people poking into their business, least of all a murderer." The warning sounded harsh, unlike Buzz. On the other hand, when had we ever had occasion to discuss a murder. He released my shoulder and wove his large fingers around a strand of my springy hair. "Once a person has killed," he added, "it's not a big deal to do it again."

I shivered. "Could we talk about Cruz'n Cuisine?"

If Buzz was surprised or put off, I couldn't tell. "Fortier screwed me," he said flatly. "Just like he did the rest of the kitchen." He snorted. This was more than he'd been willing to say in five months.

Fortier's womanizing disgusted Buzz more than Fortier's theft. How was it possible that this man was single, with not even a significant other?

"What happened, exactly?"

"Am I a suspect?" He attempted a return to light banter, but he lost interest in my hair.

"At this point, aren't we all?"

Whomever the police might suspect, I didn't think I'd suffered some temporary amnesia during which I'd acted out a latent fantasy to kill Fortier. It was equally hard to believe that Buzz Fraser had done it. But if I wanted to investigate, I needed more to go on than gut instinct.

Since we couldn't see anything from the balcony, we backed against the railing and watched the party through the French doors.

"So you want to know the details of my motive?" Buzz asked.

"Give me a break, Buzz." He had not quite regained his kidding tone. "I'm new at this." The cold had increased my hunger, and I nervously bit into the sponge cake layered with goo. This new endeavor of mine could make enemies and alienate people.

"Okay, Carol. I don't know how it happened. I made the pitch. Everything was going great. Then the station manager dropped me like a hot potato."

"In Eldon's hand," I quipped, a standard kitchen joke. Most of us had scarred, heat resistant hands, whereas Eldon's were renowned for dainty softness.

"Like that," Buzz said. "I thought he'd changed his mind about the program." He shrugged.

I set the plate of cake crumbs on the rail and squeezed Buzz. "Do you have any idea why the station manager replaced you?"

He flinched. "My alcohol problem."

I knew about this vaguely. Unlike Fortier, trained by the Culinary Academy, Buzz had learned the trade on the job, starting at the kitchen of a camp, an extension of a dry-out clinic.

"You've been clean a long time, haven't you?"

"I got a D.U.I. last year, Carol."

"I didn't know that." I felt queasy. Maybe getting to the bottom of things wasn't all it was cracked up to be.

"Right after the party."

Last year's party had featured a huge, crystal, never-empty punch bowl right where the shrimp were now. Chad and I had come by cab and I'd been somewhere between tipsy and inebriated, but even so I remembered the raucous knot of guys on the balcony. I'd had to restrain Chad from joining them. Big Red, the cook, had shouted, "Geronimo," and leaped. Then there'd been the ambulance.

Since Big Red had only broken his leg and seemed to enjoy being the center of attention, people laughed and joked about the party for weeks. The whole affair had been stupid, but fun. Now, I glimpsed a sadder side, the temptation the party offered to someone like Buzz.

I shook off the guilt. Buzz could have called a cab. I knew why he hadn't, though. He had fallen off the wagon. Buzz did not like to screw up. He had wanted to escape, unnoticed.

"I had some counseling," Buzz said.

I'd been quiet too long.

"I'm not drinking." His voice sounded unsure, as though the habit were a capricious monkey, tamed and housebroken, but never controlled.

I pinched up the last bits of the petit four and licked them from my fingertips. "If I didn't know about your D.U.I., how did Fortier?"

"I'm not sure he knew, Carol. After all, when did Fortier ever need facts?"

"But you think he suggested to the station manager you might not be reliable, that you had an alcohol problem?"

"That's what I think. Then I think Fortier turned on his charm, pulled out his credentials, and said, 'I'm your man,' and it was a done deal."

"You don't sound bitter." In spite of the brisk night air, I felt clammy and nauseous. Saliva pooled in my mouth.

"Oh, I'm bitter." His body tensed. "I've never been any good at expressing stuff. But I feel it with a vengeance." His right hand balled into a fist. His voice was steely. "I could have killed Fortier. Easily."

"But you didn't," I blurted, feeling uncomfortable. This was not the Buzz Fraser I knew. "Did you?"

He pointed through the glass at the package in Eldon's hand. "Come on. Let's go in. That's your present."

Instead, I twisted over the railing and heaved, grateful for the screen of fog.

CHAPTER FOURTEEN

When I crawled out of bed the next morning, Chad brought me a large mug of black French roast.

"Aren't you going to roof today?" I asked. Reinforced by a jolt of caffeine, I stumbled toward the bathroom.

"I thought I'd do something special for you on your day off." He'd been asleep when I had come home and had no way to know how weak I felt.

I pressed a steaming washcloth to my face. Vomiting was a violent act and even after a night's rest, I felt as wobbly as a colt. Buzz had been great, fetching my gift, a glass of water, and damp napkins. I contrasted Buzz's care with Chad's state of ignorance, and quite unfairly, found Chad lacking.

But I couldn't tell Chad what had happened. He might conclude, as I had, that someone had tried to poison me. Dealing with Chad's protective reaction was more than I wanted to take on.

"Why?" I asked him, but the cloth muffled my question.

I pulled away the cloth. Chad and Buzz were about the same age, but Chad looked twenty-five rather than thirty-five. He had the exuberance of a teenager, although at the moment his face sagged with a crestfallen expression. Perhaps because I felt weary, I longed for the stolid, older presence of Buzz.

"Why not?" Chad watched me brush my teeth. "Why not take the love of my life on a romantic getaway?"

"That's really thoughtful." I tried to sound enthusiastic around a mouthful of toothpaste. It was hard to connect "love of my life" with the pallid face and Bozo-the-Clown hair in the mirror. And a "romantic getaway" could put a damper on my snooping.

I continued brushing my teeth, stalling further discussion. Chad watched from the doorway as though my foaming mouth were sexy.

My mind spun away from his proposal toward murder and suspects. Alexis had implied that Julieanne Fortier still loved Jean Alcee, but that only increased the likelihood she'd killed him. No wrath like that of a woman scorned. Good grief, I sounded like my mother. I spit and rinsed my mouth. Chad continued to stand there, waiting for a response. I couldn't force my mind back to his topic. Instead I was thinking about Kris Kringle gifts.

I did not believe Fortier had participated in the gift exchange, but Eldon insisted that Fortier had received a jar of honey decorated with a holiday ribbon. He'd told the detectives about it and they'd taken the information seriously.

To forestall my talk with Chad, I examined my weary face in the mirror. Not bad. I looked okay with pale skin and even the bloodshot whites of my eyes threw the blue-green irises into high relief.

The cops had spent an hour searching for the elusive jar of honey. Anyone could have given the gift to Jean Alcee Fortier, including Julieanne. Alexis could have delivered it for her. Maybe they'd both benefit from his death. That's if the jar even existed. Maybe Eldon had invented it to divert attention from the kitchen's food.

Chad pushed away from the doorframe. "I could tell the CD player didn't surprise you."

"I love it." I slipped on my rose-colored, terry robe.

"I know you like it, but it wasn't a surprise."

We walked to the kitchen. "That's okay, Chad. I don't need to be surprised."

He put the cast iron skillet on a burner, slid down the cutting board from the top of the refrigerator, and chopped onion, garlic and green pepper.

Our tiny maple table had two drop leaves that we kept folded. The menorah sat in the table's center, my present from Chad's mom. I hadn't gotten her anything, but Chad had bought her something and signed the card from both of us. I pulled out a caned chair from one end. In the event of company, we raised the leaves and hauled down two chairs from the attic.

"Who gave you the book?" Chad asked.

"My Kris Kringle." *Armed and Dangerous,* the perfect gift, lay on the freestanding counter. It was a companion book of *Deadly Doses.* My mind drifted back to Buzz, the party, and the murder. I wanted to know for certain whether the honey was a legitimate Kringle gift or not. Especially since it had disappeared. I could figure out whether the honey was a Kringle gift by seeing who had participated, who had drawn whom, and whether everyone was matched when I finished.

Chad cracked eggs into a bowl. "Who was your Kris Kringle?"

"Just who you guessed."

He tossed the chopped vegetables into the skillet. They sizzled in hot oil. His back stayed to me.

Chad was predictable. He was chewing on the way I'd discouraged his attendance of the party. I didn't reassure him. Jealousy was a wild beast, not reined by logic. Any protestations about Buzz and me would only spur the ride.

All week I'd innocently raved about my Kris Kringle gifts. I'd discovered them on my refrigerator shelf, in my locker, and taped to the antenna of my car. "Must be Suzanne," I'd said.

"It's Buzz," Chad had insisted with the intuition of a bared heart.

At the time, I'd shrugged, unsure, or not wanting to deal with it.

The gifts had been intimate, like the large, tortoise shell hair clip. This was someone who knew I wouldn't care for the popular, elasticized ruffles, who knew only a large clip would hold my heavy hair, who sensed I might like to clip my hair although I braided it for work.

Chad added the eggs to the skillet, pressed wheat bread into the toaster, and shredded Monterey Jack cheese.

"So where are we going on our romantic getaway?"

He turned and beamed. "It's a surprise."

Chad drove my car rather than his beat-up Ford Ranger, and

we headed south on coastal Freeway 1. Out my window, wooded hills studded with houses fell away to the ocean. The overcast sky obscured the outline of Monterey Peninsula curving into the Pacific.

I could have gotten out of the trip if I'd told Chad I'd been sick. I dismissed the idea again. He'd worry too much.

I could count the times I'd thrown up (at least the times I remembered) on one hand. When I'd left for the party, I had felt fine. At the party, I hadn't eaten anything but one petit four and there wasn't much in sponge cake and sugar that could go bad. A case of food poisoning seemed out of the question.

"Is something wrong?" Chad asked.

"No, nothing, sweetheart." In spite of the cold, morning fog, I'd rolled down the window. If Chad could intuit something was wrong from my back, I didn't dare look at him.

"You looked pale this morning."

"Tired," I replied, as I concluded all over again that someone had tried to poison me. But why? And if he were going to bother, why not kill me? Whoever our murderer was, he certainly knew how to kill if that's what he wanted.

"That's what I thought," Chad said.

For a moment I imagined Chad was agreeing with my conclusion. I'd lost track of our conversation.

"A relaxing trip is just what you need. Get away from the house. The chores."

I barely comprehended what he was saying. I recalled Santa Claus, or Eldon as Santa Claus. He had been specific. The pink petit four had been made especially for Alexis. Not me. Alexis had swapped it for my chocolate one.

"Enjoying the view?" Chad asked.

"Oh yes, beautiful."

Why would Eldon want to poison Alexis? None of this made sense. If the petit four had been poisoned with whatever had killed Fortier, I should be dead. If the petit four had been doctored, it must have been with something different, like an emetic. Not lethal, but enough to make a person sick. But why would anyone want to make Alexis sick? Maybe Fortier's murder had unleashed my imagination, that part of me that invented bad screenplays, and in reality, a weird flu had seized me.

"What's wrong?" Chad asked. "You're acting like someone obsessed. Or possessed."

When I turned toward him, I didn't see his face. There, dividing the north and south bound lanes, were rows of oleander bushes. Free, available, and very toxic. If I remembered correctly from my reference book, oleander poisoning produced the flu-like symptoms Jean had experienced. I couldn't wait to get home and double check this idea. If the symptoms were a match, I'd consider an anonymous phone call to the police. So what if it was far-fetched. Pathologists could detect almost any poison, but it helped if they knew what to look for.

I lay a hand on Chad's thigh to reassure him. "I am obsessed."

Chad exited the freeway on 152 through downtown Watsonville, much recovered from the Loma Prieta earthquake of 1989. Main Street had preserved its turn-of-the-century, western flavor. The new Ford's Department Store, a gray block with orange trim and too few windows, occupied a corner of a central intersection.

It was the downtown's anchor store. At a diagonal, across the intersection, a familiar figure lounged on a bench at the plaza.

"Pull over!" I stuck my body far out the window like a rowdy teenager, and waved over the top of the car. "Abundio!" He looked around. "Over here, Abundio!"

Chad drove across the intersection, but construction had torn up any possibility of parking on that section of Main Street. "Why do you want to stop?" he asked in frustration.

"Talk to Abundio." I looked back. The tall, young dishwasher gazed into the cloudy sky, as though contemplating whether he'd heard the voice of God.

"Doesn't he have an alibi?"

Chad didn't circle the block, and I didn't protest.

"Do you think that's the only reason I'd want to talk to someone?"

"Yeah," Chad said. "Lately, that's what I think."

I sighed. We crossed the dried out Pajaro River and continued down into Pajaro. Dilapidated wooden buildings hugged the ground and advertised *pan dulce* and *cerveza*, sweet bread and beer. I did wonder about Abundio. He'd slipped out the back at the sound of sirens, and had remained invisible that entire morning, with Victor scrambling to cover for him.

Besides irritating my co-workers and endangering myself, I realized my investigation might lead to marital discord. But that wouldn't alter my course. I agonized over decisions, but once made, I seldom changed my mind. My mother called this obstinate. I called it persistent.

The small town gave way to the fertile, low lying Pajaro Valley, nurseries and fields. At Prunedale, Chad took Freeway 101 south. Prunedale nestled in the hills to the west. It was a small community and I'd never been there, but it seemed to make local news an inordinate number of times with brush fires, marijuana fields, or substandard camps for migrant workers. In my mind, it was a place for renegades.

After Salinas, 101 flattened into a warm, monotonous stretch to Soledad, where Chad exited and drove like he was looking for something.

"Oh, goodie. A tour of the prison," I joked. "Chad, how did you ever guess?"

He didn't smile. As a matter of fact, his mouth turned down, as though he thought I may have preferred the prison tour to whatever he had planned. He stopped at Burger King for lunch. Since he'd packed drinks and snacks, it seemed like a suspense-creating diversion. Or, maybe he couldn't go any longer without nicotine. He grabbed a package of Vantage from his shirt pocket before the car door thunked.

After I'd eaten a salad and he'd downed a Whopper and fries, he doubled back on the thoroughfare, turned on a two-lane highway and headed into the parched rolling hills. Scrub oaks dotted the chaparral country, my favorite kind.

I'd deduced from an inconspicuous sign that we were on our way to Pinnacles National Monument. Since I'd never been there, my curiosity stirred. The land did not look like it could contain pinnacles. The narrow road through private pastures and over cattle guards certainly didn't lead to any tourist mecca. It was eerily quiet. We didn't pass another car.

The pinnacles appeared suddenly, solid, rocky interruptions of a gentle landscape. Chad pulled into a parking lot. Besides restrooms, a ranger's station and a few picnic tables, the place remained undeveloped.

"Like it?" he asked.

I climbed out, stretched, looked at the few cars in the lot, heard the ugly caw of a jay, distinct and separate in the quiet, and sniffed the sagey air heightened by the smell of much needed coming rain.

"I love it!"

"Better than *Armed and Dangerous*?"

"Love trumps murder."

CHAPTER FIFTEEN

Four o'clock in the morning was an obscene time to be at work. On autopilot, I climbed the steps to the loading dock, entered the hallway, punched in, and changed into my uniform. I dragged myself up the hallway and into the kitchen. My bakery was off to the side, but I didn't stop there. I passed through the kitchen, turning left before the pastry department.

I unlocked the first refrigerator, feeling gloomy that we'd had to resort to padlocks after the meat thefts last Christmas. Since I was first to arrive, Eldon trusted me with access to the key.

Outside it poured, a great day to snuggle in bed with Chad. Instead, I irritably shoved aside a half-gallon of black olives and a block of feta cheese parked on my shelf. They should have been on the chefs' Use-First shelf, but a quick look up told me there wasn't room. I'd bitch later to Eldon. Maybe, if the door weren't always locked, someone would use the stuff, or, at least, clean the shelf.

As I lugged my five-gallon bucket of dough and "borrowed" a scoop from the garde manger, I thought of the bed and breakfast in Carmel where Chad had taken me after our hike. We'd dined on our provisions and the fresh fruit and sherry in the room. And that night, in our haven, we'd listened to the promise and thrum of rain.

I snapped chocolate chip balls on the cookie sheets in rapid-fire motion. Ching, ching, ching. I fantasized about myself with limpid eyes, Chad's strong, warm hand on my soft belly. I should quit my job, overcome my silly obsession with crime, and have a couple of kids with this dreamy man before time ran out. I resented coming back to this place where someone was mean enough to put an emetic in a petit four. *Where someone is deranged enough to murder*, I corrected myself.

On the other hand, I may not have been slamming cookies on the tray because of my return to work, but rather because I'd been seduced away from it. I had lost the momentum of my "investigation." I wasn't sure what the point of it was. I had even forgotten to look up oleander. My current situation brought up the age-old, annoying issue of how one held on to self in relationships. Quit my job and depend on someone else? Kids? This wasn't for me. Holy moley.

While it'd been enjoyable, no, more than that—supremely delicious—to have Buzz's sweetness inspire Chad to such heights, I could see Chad's jealousy developing into a real mess.

I carried the empty bowl around the corner to Victor and Abundio.

"*Buenos dias, amigos.*"

"Such generosity," Victor said, rinsing the huge, sticky, stainless steel bowl.

Abundio held up a wet, soapy hand. He was tall and skinny, with lots of freckles, reddish-brown hair, and a big grin. He and Victor didn't look like relatives, but whole strings of people at Archibald's were. Nepotism ran rampant.

"Eh, Carol, know why cannibals won't eat clowns?" Victor asked.

I shook my head.

"Dey tas' funny."

I smiled, ducked back into my niche, and continued to mull over my personal life. I couldn't blame Chad for feeling a bit insecure. With his family, I considered it miraculous that Chad was normal.

"Carol."

I jumped and turned.

"Sorry."

Delores stood in the entrance. Her large, thick-lashed eyes looked red and puffy. With her dark hair and brown skin, her blue eyes always startled me a little, even though from Abundio's red hair and freckles, it was clear fairness ran in the family's genes.

"Whatcha need, Delores?"

She stared at the table, then at the floor. When she raised her head, she looked haunted and ineffably sad, like a deserted child.

How did Fortier do this? How did a middle-aged chef command such power over a stunningly beautiful girl?

"The melon baller?" she asked.

I glanced guiltily at the doughy scoop at the end of my table.

"Tell Suzanne I'm sorry. I thought I'd be done with it before you missed it. I didn't think we served melons in December."

A tear leaked down Delores' smooth cheek.

"Oh, sweetie...." My heart ached for her. I stopped myself from saying Fortier wasn't worth it, and instead grabbed the folding steps from the hall. "Sit down. Have a good cry."

Her blue eyes widened at the sight of the steps, but she complied. I handed her one of the ubiquitous, small white towels, and noticed a glow-in-the-dark Band-Aid on her plump thumb. But, she didn't cry anymore.

"I better get back before Suzanne gets mad."

"Suzanne will not get mad."

Of everyone in the kitchen, Suzanne had the most even temper. She was the only one of us that I'd describe as sweet. Even Delores had flared up when she thought Fortier's eyes were roving, as no doubt they had been. How did a possessive twenty-year-old deal with the fact her boyfriend had once been her mom's lover, I wondered.

"Are you okay?" Delores asked.

"I just had a surprising thought." I didn't tell Delores it was about her. What if she had recently learned about her mom and Fortier? I didn't know exactly when Fortier had been with Esperanza, but it had been a long time ago. Delores would have been a child, maybe even a baby. Esperanza struck me as a private, discreet person. It was possible that she had never told Delores, that Delores had learned about the relationship the way everybody else did—through kitchen gossip. Could such a discovery provoke a fiery, jealous girl to kill? I reminded myself of my basic contention:

anyone could kill if the circumstances were right. I was back in the groove and my mood felt lighter.

I did a quick look-see into the kitchen. Eldon hovered by a frantic Ray on the front line. The front line demanded more skill and timing than the mass cooking in the back line, and Ray had not been properly trained. Like several others, he'd been tossed into his new position by Fortier's death and was learning the job under pressure.

In spite of Eldon's preoccupation, he could bounce over to the bakery at any moment. "Let's give Suzanne the melon baller and punch out for an official break."

Delores agreed. "No offense, Carol, but this room gives me the creeps."

The whole kitchen was a little creepy given that a murder might have occurred here. How Eldon had kept it running without a hitch spoke to his managerial skill. In my imagination his coup involved the CEO of the conference center speaking to someone in power about 600 plates a day at fifty dollars a plate.

We entered the Employees Dining Room where Suzanne's cousin had been hired to fill Big Red's place as he moved into the main kitchen. Even before Fortier's death, the kitchen operated on the burn-and-turn principle: Burn 'em out and turn 'em over.

Delores and I filled paper cups full of coffee and Delores picked up a couple of my overdone spice cookies that'd been relegated to EDR. We sat in the corner furthest from the steam table.

I launched right in. "Would you happen to know the last thing Fortier ate before he died?"

A blush rose from the top of her chef's smock to the bottom

of her white hat. The question had been blunt, but I didn't see anything embarrassing about it.

"I meant food," I stammered, feeling like an idiot. "Do you know what food he ate last? Excluding the *lebkuchen* dough he may have sampled."

She nodded, and the blush deepened a shade.

Now I was confused. "Well, what?"

She squinched her face and squirmed in her seat.

"Tell me," I coaxed.

She shook her head.

"Come on. I won't tell anyone."

"Honey," she croaked.

I nodded, eager and waiting.

Delores scooted the cafeteria chair closer and whispered, "We went in the walk-in cooler."

This particular Fortier ploy had become part of the initiation rite for every female employee. Many years ago, for me, it had been instructive. When Fortier had led me from the cooler, I'd felt the half dozen sets of eyes staring at my nipples, and since then I'd managed, in spite of Fortier's good looks, abundant energy, and impressive knowledge of cooking, never to forget how juvenile he could be. My vigilance didn't prevent incidents like the one in the locker room, but I'd circumvented a lot by not being alone with the guy and not passing him in the tighter spots of the kitchen. I felt guilty for not warning Delores, when on her first day, she had emerged in the puff of cold fog, asking about the labels, oblivious to the guys checking out her chest.

"At first it was like a picnic," Delores continued. She had no discernible accent, but her voice had a muted quality, a lack of explosive b's and p's, probably learned from her mother. "He was eating the honey on your scones, but he said they were bitter like you didn't stir in the soda good." Delores lowered her eyes.

I thought badly of the dead. The nerve of him saying my scones were bitter!

"Then..." She blushed again. "He wanted to put the honey on my..." She giggled, the nervous sound of a modest person. Her hands fluttered around her lap. "I couldn't."

Part of her embarrassment seemed to stem from her inability to accommodate Fortier. Hatred of the guy erupted in me like torched kerosene. He'd taken an innocent young lady and made her feel ashamed of her purity.

"But he did eat more honey?" I pressed.

She winced. "From my nipples."

CHAPTER SIXTEEN

I glanced at the clock up on the wall behind the steam table. "We'd better get back." We were entitled to two fifteen-minute breaks. I was enough of a one-person show to take them back-to-back, but Delores was new and vulnerable. She couldn't afford for Eldon to write her up.

We tucked our paper cups into the garbage can. "Did Fortier get sick right after that?"

"I think so. We can't see the line chefs from the garde manger, and we're not on the route to the bathroom."

"When did you guys go into the cooler?"

She reddened and shrugged. "Mid-morning?"

I made a mental note to ask Eldon about how and when Fortier had first gotten sick.

We left the cafeteria and entered the tacky hallway used only by employees. We passed the employee restrooms and locker room. I pushed at the swinging door into the kitchen.

"Who gave him the honey?" I asked.

"I think *Tio* Victor."

I paused with my hand on the door into the kitchen and shushed her. This was a new twist. We were about to enter near the dishwashers, but Delores hadn't shown the slightest hesitancy in mentioning Victor.

"Why you want me to be quiet?" she whispered.

She evidently had not grasped the possible connection between the honey and Fortier's death. However, the murderer certainly knew the connection and might not appreciate others making it.

I backed away from the door, so it wouldn't swing back out and hit me in the face.

"*Tio* Victor keeps bees," she explained in a low voice, baffled by my behavior.

I nudged her into the supply room at the end of the hall. "Promise me you'll keep our conversation a secret."

"Gawd," she said, wrinkling her nose. "You think I'm gonna tell people 'bout that?"

"Don't tell anybody about any of it."

I wondered if my advice could be considered an obstruction to justice. Certainly Delores should tell the police. I could not imagine her Uncle Victor giving Fortier anything but a sock in the jaw. If he had given the honey to Fortier, it would have been to kill him.

"Are you sure the honey was from Victor?"

"It was a Kris Kringle present." She frowned and picked at the Band-Aid on her thumb. "We sorta got in a fight about it because Jean wouldn't let me see the tag."

"Tag?" I asked excitedly.

"On the ribbon. Jean told me it was from his secret admirer. He did that to make me mad, I know."

I realized why she hadn't connected the honey and the death. She wasn't dumb. She was too innocent to imagine murder. She might be in for a shock when the police reported the autopsy results. To her, Fortier's death had been an inexplicable act of God. I dismissed my earlier idea of her as a suspect.

"Delores, what happened to the jar of honey?"

"I don't know. I left first."

Something was happening to me. My heart banged. Adrenaline and endorphins shot like starbursts through my body. The excitement was like a drug rush. The missing jar of honey could be a solid piece of evidence. The police had looked for it, but half-heartedly. At the time, there'd been no direct link between it and Fortier's death.

My mind raced. What if Fortier knew he'd been poisoned, had sat on my stool because he could go no farther, and put his finger in my dough, not to sample it, but rather, knowing it was full of molasses and honey, to point at it, a desperate, last minute message? Nah, I thought. I had been reading too many mysteries.

Delores's gaze switched across my face a couple of times and then ran over the wire shelves, the stacks of plates and trays. "I really should get back to work."

I was blocking the girl's path from the supply room to the swinging doors. "Just out of curiosity, Delores, whose name did you draw in the Kris Kringle?"

"Patsy," she said. "Actually I drew Suzanne's name, but Eldon wanted to switch."

That made sense. Eldon would be at a loss for what to get Patsy. On the other hand, his eyes tracked Suzanne whenever she trotted across the kitchen.

I pushed open the door. "Who had your name, Delores?"

"Ray."

I wanted to know if the jar of honey could have been a Kris Kringle present. If so, who had drawn Fortier's name? I couldn't imagine Fortier participating in the gift exchange, but if he hadn't, wouldn't he wonder about an unexpected gift? With his ego, maybe not. According to Delores, there had been a tag on the jar. Could it really have been from Victor?

All through my shift, I stayed wired as though on a double espresso. After that, I returned to the EDR for lunch. I saw the room and the people as though for the first time. A line filed before the shiny stainless steel table with its Plexiglas sneeze guards. The aromas of leftover prime rib and horseradish crowded the small, warm room. I knew most of the employees only vaguely, since most were from the on-coming shift. I started and finished earlier than my co-workers. However, Buzz stood in line, in uniform, taking a late break. He turned and winked at me. My heart did a weird little soft shoe with cane and top hat.

Since the party, something had changed in our relationship, and I didn't like it. I wanted the good old days when a wink was just a wink.

I slid a plastic plate from the shelf, but waved people ahead of me as I stalled, hoping Alexis would show. Being stubborn and obsessive, I needed to let go of my initial suspicion of Julieanne—and, maybe, by extension, Alexis—before I could focus on this new twist—the honey from the supposed Kris Kringle. Uncle Victor?

I had shed my uniform and slipped on rose-colored sweats, but the tight braid of my hair pulled on my scalp. I looked forward to the tingling pleasure of its release. My mouth salivated at the smell of the succulent meat, until I remembered the last time I'd eaten at work—the petit four at the party. Nausea fluttered through my belly.

The guy at the end of the line turned to me. "Dead meat." He wrinkled his nose.

"Do you prefer it pulsating?" The line moved and I hung back.

"I guess you don't feel like eating either," he said.

He was thin and anemic-looking. In truth, I thought most Americans ate too much red meat, but this guy's attitude was annoying. And in his case, some red meat might do him good. Plus prime rib was tasty.

"We have incisors for ripping meat from bone."

"Oh, one of those," the cadaver said. He stepped forward and inspected the cases for dead plants to eat.

I made a face at his back. I was standing on tiptoes to see how much prime rib remained when Alexis hustled into the room, in uniform but out of breath. I stepped into the line. Preoccupied with the clock, she grabbed a plate and stood behind me.

I turned. "Hi, Alexis."

"Oh, hi, Carol." She jiggled the plate in one hand. The fingers of the other rubbed at her thumbnail.

I inched forward and spooned rosemary potatoes onto my

plate. In *sotto voce*, I said, "I was very interested in our discussion the other night."

Alexis glanced around the room and spotted Buzz at a table. She nearly dropped her plate.

I tonged broccoli flowers and Alexis followed suit. "I was hoping I could meet Julieanne. Talk to her."

"She left."

"Left?" I echoed. Her action screamed guilty like a neon pink sign. It seemed abrupt, a definite reaction. On the other hand, my progress had been sluggish. Ten days had passed since Fortier had been murdered in the bakery. I also had the nagging detail of the honey. If it had been the vehicle, how had Julieanne gotten the poisoned product into the kitchen? How had she known to disguise it as a Kringle present?

"She went back to New Orleans," Alexis said.

I wondered what the cops would make of that.

Alexis forked a slab of meat onto her plate, placed it on a tray, and gathered silverware. Her gaze flicked over the nearly full room, to where Buzz sat alone. I wondered if she'd get up the courage to sit with him, and where I could go if she did. As Alexis remained mired in personal crisis, her guard down, I asked, "Do you know who'll inherit Jean's condo?"

"Me." She looked up at me, her eyes fearful, but whether about the condo or sitting with Buzz, I didn't know. I led the way to his table, deciding to eat fast so the two would be alone.

"Did your uncle leave a will?"

"What?" Her fingers tightened on her tray.

I pitied her. No member of the opposite sex had ever reduced me to a bumbling stupor, although I'd once had a confusing crush on a guy, who I later realized was my brother Donald's first boyfriend.

"A will?" I prodded, as we seated ourselves at Buzz's table. Buzz and I exchanged glances. Alexis said nothing. I felt like kicking her. I did. Fast and friendly under the table.

"No, uhm," she said, as though prodded from a slumber. "He had one of those things, a living trust." Resentful eyes locked on mine.

So she knew Fortier was leaving her the yacht harbor property. No wonder she'd called him generous.

I stood up with my plate. Alexis's chocolate brown eyes looked panicked. "No offense," I said, "but I've decided to eat outside."

Buzz looked at me like I was crazy, a completely logical response I realized, when I stepped into a misty rain. I gulped lunch and went home to make a phone call.

CHAPTER SEVENTEEN

As it turned out, what the police made of Julieanne's disappearance was nothing much.

"We have no reason to suspect her," the nice Detective Carman told me over the phone. Without the autopsy results, I supposed they couldn't officially suspect anyone. In the meantime, ten days had passed. Today was the 29th. The killer had had a lot of time to cover his or her tracks. He could have disposed of the honey a long time ago.

Detective Carman thanked me. I grabbed my book *Deadly Doses* and wandered to the backyard, feeling like an idiot. Had I expected them to send a posse galloping to New Orleans to drag Julieanne back to Santa Cruz? They barely had the staff to deal with everyday burglaries and obvious murders like the shooting on the West Side.

If only gangs could practice restraint, I thought. Poison would be so much more efficient than drive-by shootings. With a little arsenic, the Watsonville rival gangs of Northside and Poorside could wipe out one another, and the whole affair might be passed off as a bad batch of chorizo.

In our tiny backyard, as in the front, Chad and I had foregone any attempt at a lawn and had opted for an English garden, a flagstone path through wildflowers and drought-resistant perennials. Along the redwood fence hung baskets of fuchsias, chenille plants, and pelargoniums.

I lounged on the brick landing. Lola snuck up on me, as though she might startle me away, and curled around my butt. Her caution had no doubt developed because I hopped up to do "things" in a manner that mystified even my husband.

Chad had hoisted Lola from a free box at the flea market because he felt sorry for her. Back then, I'd made some snide comment about picking the ugliest kitten he could find.

Now I scratched under her pink flea collar. "Lola, you are so cute." And she was.

She purred and squeezed her round green eyes shut in ecstasy, then stretched, arching, as if to say, "Of course."

With my perverse aversion to tables of contents, I leafed through *Deadly Doses*. I found oleander under Poisonous Plants, Quickly Fatal, after monkshood and before paternoster pea. In Sanskrit the plant's name meant "Horse Killer," in Arabic and Italian "Ass Killer." Well, that was appropriate.

Could the killer have selected the poison for its meaning? The twisted wit appealed to me, but I couldn't imagine anyone, except maybe myself, doing something like that in real life.

On a scale of one to six, nerium oleander had a toxicity of six with a reaction time of twenty to forty minutes. A native of Asia, it had been introduced as an ornamental shrub in the United States. All parts were deadly, including the nectar of the flower, smoke from a burning plant, or water in which the flowers had been placed.

The drug stimulated the heart, causing sweating, vomiting, bloody diarrhea, unconsciousness, respiratory paralysis and death.

In Europe, oleander was used as rat poison.

The next line popped my eyes. When bees used oleander pollen for their honey, the honey could be poisonous.

Maybe there was no mystery at all. Victor, the patriarch of the Medina family, felt protective of Delores. He made certain his bees sucked up oleander nectar. Then, he slipped Fortier, the womanizer, the ass, a jar of his special product.

CHAPTER EIGHTEEN

I didn't want to talk to Eldon. My reluctance had nothing to do with the petit four that made me puke. I doubted Eldon had doctored it. I was curious why he'd claimed it was his work and I wondered if it had a connection to the murder. But I dreaded the conversation. Eldon had no life except Archibald's. He tended to be officious and long-winded. And he was my boss.

As far as I knew, Eldon didn't take breaks, and he ate his lunch in the mid-afternoon during the lull in customers. However, he arrived about six and ate breakfast before his shift. Knowing this, the next morning I caught Eldon in the EDR hunched over three pieces of French toast swimming in maple syrup. He had one of my leftover apricot Danishes on the side and a cup of coffee that looked as though it were half cream. I bet it had three or four sugars in it.

I got a cup of coffee and straddled a chair at his table, my elbows on its back. I wanted the little physical barrier between us. The position also made it easier to hop up. "One quick question, Eldon."

He made a motion for me to turn the chair and patted the table, but I acted ignorant of sign language. He chewed meticulously, swallowed, and dabbed his mouth. "You have fifteen minutes, Carol. Relax." He saw no irony in his statement. With his fork and knife he cut a perfect, fat wedge of French toast. "I've been thinking of organizing a stress management workshop for the employees. I've noticed that some of the staff have been very stressed by what happened."

What happened? Talk about glossing over—no mention of Fortier or death, not even a euphemism like passed away.

"Delores, in particular, although she's not the only one. Esperanza seems distraught as well. Have you noticed?"

Distraught was too histrionic for the stoic Esperanza. "She's probably worried about Delores," I said.

"Buzz, too," he said, twirling a forkful of cooked bread in the syrup.

Two words. Buzz, too. That was completely unlike Eldon. I looked at him, but he watched back. We both tried to read the other. "Buzz seems distraught?"

"I guess you haven't noticed...." His voice drifted, but as I opened my mouth to pop my question, he added, "You seem a little hyper yourself, Carol."

"I'm okay," I said.

"I know this group from San Jose. They're very good for upbeat presentations. Professional, but not beyond our budget."

I waited as he more firmly speared the goo-soaked wedge in preparation to lift it.

"I attended one of their seminars called 'Stress for Success.'"

"Interesting concept," I muttered.

That was the wrong thing to say, but I could hardly tell my boss to shut up and listen while I asked him one simple question.

"It is an interesting concept," he said. "It focused on how to convert stress into motivation and drive, rather than how to get rid of stress." He drove the wedge of French toast through the brown puddle as though it were a toy boat. "I think I could get Archibald's to spring for the cost." The bread went round and round in the brown puddle. He didn't plan to pop it into his mouth until he finished talking, which could be the next blue moon. "We could probably—"

"Eldon," I said, "excuse me. I'm sorry to interrupt, but I have to get back to work."

He glanced at his digital watch. "You still have seven minutes, Carol." He stuck the French toast into his mouth.

"When and how did Fortier get sick?"

His light brown eyes looked at me as the smooth, pale face moved with his patient, thorough chewing.

"I'm surprised the incident has agitated you so much, Carol. I mean, certainly, it was a shock for everyone, but I didn't think you and Fortier were friendly, actually the opposite. I frankly don't believe the police's insinuations, but if I had to choose someone, to well, ehm, …." He cleared his throat.

I restrained from clutching my forehead and moaning. Usually I escaped these "conversations" by leaving, but now I needed information. "When did Fortier get sick?" I persisted.

"Right after his break," Eldon said. "He and Delores were in the cooler, fooling around." He smacked his lips, furrowed his brow, and shook his head at their behavior.

I was stunned to hear Eldon make such a personal remark. "Didn't you mind?"

He shrugged. "They both punched out. If a guy's going through a mid-life crisis and needs to act like a teenager, as long as he does it on his time, that's his problem."

"And how did he get sick?"

"Well, in spite of the police's insinuations, I never thought for a moment, Carol, that it was caused by our kitchen or your *lebkuchen*. I don't think he got sick from something he ate. Their suggestions have been bad for our kitchen's morale. That's why I think this workshop—"

"Eldon," I interrupted.

His smooth forehead puckered, and, almost as a reflex, he checked his watch.

"Eldon," I said again, feeling frantic. "I meant how was Fortier sick. Did he vomit or what?"

Eldon wrinkled his nose. "He was sweating and his breathing was ragged. He said he felt sick and needed to go home. I offered to call a taxi. I really didn't think he should try to drive, but then he rushed off. I assumed to the restroom and I assumed to vomit. I didn't see him after that. Until, of course, Patsy found him."

He checked his watch.

"Thanks," I said. "Oh, yeah, Eldon, would you tell the cooks to keep their use-first stuff off my shelf?" Before he could reply, I bailed.

CHAPTER NINETEEN

"Ah shit," I said aloud, as I went out the EDR door. I was the world's worst investigator. I hadn't managed to ask him a thing about the petit four and I'd forgotten to ask Eldon about his Kris Kringle. I knew he'd exchanged with Delores to get Suzanne's name, but who'd drawn his name?

If I could determine who'd given Fortier the present, I'd be a step closer to solving the mystery. Delores thought the honey was her Uncle Victor's, but she may have jumped to that conclusion simply because he kept bees. Or did the jar have distinguishing characteristics? Even so, the murderer could have used Victor's honey to point suspicion at Victor.

Eldon's description of Fortier's symptoms fit my reference book's descriptions of oleander poisoning. My guess was that the killer had put oleander in the honey, possibly via bees, and Fortier had been murdered with sweetness. He'd licked the ambrosia from the horns of plenty and was very sick by the time he walked to the kitchen.

In the cold hallway, I shivered. Killing someone with a Christmas gift seemed cold-blooded, even to me. The aroma of my garlic/rosemary bread wafted down the tiled corridor. Under the pungent bouquet, the basic smell of baking bread comforted me. Breathing it in, I felt calmer.

I contemplated the phone in the hall. I wanted to make my anonymous tip now, before I lost my nerve. I went into the restroom, yanked down a paper towel, and returned to the phone. I pulled up the unwieldy directory by its chain, balanced it on a raised knee, and looked up the number for the tip line. The book said "anonymous crime information," but I wasn't taking any chances. Feeling like a gangster, I covered the mouthpiece with the paper towel. I scanned the hallway as I listened to the recorded message in English and then in Spanish. When I heard the beep, I blurted that the police should have the pathologist working on the Fortier case check for oleander poisoning.

I slammed down the receiver and wiped my sweaty palm on my hound's-tooth pants. I didn't like talking on the phone in the best of circumstances, which this wasn't.

When I pushed through the door into the kitchen, Abundio and Victor had arrived and were busy cleaning bowls and plates and doughy vats from the bakery. A short conveyor belt ran a rubber rack into a dishwasher, more for sterilizing than cleaning. Abundio and Victor rinsed everything first, and they grappled with the big pots and bowls by hand. They turned from their clatter and steam to greet me.

I didn't even say *hola*. "Did you guys participate in the Kris Kringle?"

They both looked startled, eyes wide and bodies quiet. To make sure he'd correctly interpreted the English, Abundio looked to Victor who repeated the question to him in Spanish. They looked quizzically at each other, and then back at me.

"Yes," Victor said, narrowing his dark eyes at me. "I had Ray's name."

That didn't, I thought, preclude him from giving Fortier a jar of honey. A sinister image of Victor formed: he lounged on a Watsonville stoop, wearing a tee shirt and baggies with a butterfly knife in the pocket. A blue bandanna wrapped his forehead, and guns filled the trunk of his lowered burgundy Impala.

I shook away the silly stereotype. This was Victor, a man with whom I'd worked for two years. The guy who told me stupid jokes.

"Who drew your name?"

He jerked a meaty thumb at Abundio. "The Kid."

Abundio grinned. A square Band-Aid covered his freckled wrist.

"What happened there?" I asked.

"Steam burn."

"Just a sec, guys." I turned the corner to check the bread. It needed about five minutes. I didn't wear a watch, for the same reason I didn't wear my wedding ring, and Eldon insisted there be no clock in the kitchen. He didn't want employees watching it. He made a point of hanging one in clear sight in the break room, though. My internal clock told me I should be mixing the dough for raspberry brioche. Instead, I broke off a piece of my aloe vera plant for Abundio.

I returned to the dishwashers. "Just one more thing." God, I sounded like Columbo. Well, I adored the rumpled sleuth, so no wonder. I handed Abundio the oozing piece of succulent, which he accepted matter-of-factly. Everyone in the kitchen humored my belief in aloe vera juice; some even swore by it. "Who drew your name, Abundio?"

His green eyes lit up. "Suzanne."

Victor reached up and playfully throttled the thin neck. "The Kid he has all the luck."

I felt a nanosecond of annoyance at the unanimous adoration of Suzanne. Surely the woman had a flaw. Perhaps she was a murderess.

I took the dozen steps back to the bakery, my head swimming with information. I needed to write it down. I flipped through my notebook, looking for an unfashionable recipe to use as scratch paper. Maybe something fried. People would rather clog their arteries with cheesecake.

Eldon caught me in the act. "The bread smells great, Carol." He sniffed elaborately. "But I don't smell any brioche."

"I was contemplating something different."

He rounded the worktable and looked over my shoulder. "Peanut butter finger crunches," he said. "Those are too much work, Carol. People love your brioche." He glanced at his watch. "But you need to get on those if we're going to have them for the breakfast bunch."

He was bouncing away when I forced myself to say, "Eldon, who drew your name for the Kris Kringle?"

The big man turned as gracefully as a ballerina. "Todd," he said. His mouth puckered as though he'd sucked a lemon. "Carol, I don't know what you're up to, but your job here is to bake, not to investigate."

"Yes, boss," I said without even a wee bit of sarcasm.

Eldon loomed in the entrance for several seconds, inspecting me. "I saw you make that call in the hall."

My heart slid to the neighborhood of my big toes, and heat squirted through my body. "I was on break."

"You went five minutes over."

I didn't know how he'd seen me, but fortunately he seemed not to have heard the call. At worst, he'd write me up. I wanted to say, "Hey, Eldon, write me up and leave me alone," but that would have left him no choice but to do it. Most of the time, like now, he only flexed his muscles. He pursed his lips and didn't say anything. The silence was disconcerting.

When he left, I pulled the recipe from its plastic sheath, but decided it would be safer if I waited until my next break to make the chart.

Later, on my second break, I used the blank side of the recipe to list the morning kitchen employees at the time of the murder. Next to their names I wrote the person to whom they'd given Kris Kringle gifts:

Carol — Esperanza

Delores — Patsy

Patsy —?

Eldon — Suzanne

Buzz — Carol

Suzanne — Abundio

Esperanza — ?

Abundio — Victor

Victor — Ray

Ray — Delores

Todd — Eldon

Fortier — ?

Big Red (then in EDR) — ?

When I looked over the chart, I felt sick. I couldn't believe any of these people had murdered Fortier, but worse than that, everyone in the kitchen had been put at risk. Anyone could have tasted the honey and died. Well, maybe not. While Fortier had cruised the kitchen, sampling everything, he'd never shared. His tightness, not his digit in my dough, had pissed me off. Yet, his niece claimed he was generous, and the insurance policy showed a financial generosity toward his wife, and he was generous with the time and attention he gave Concepción in Human Resources. People were complicated.

I sipped some water and crunched my pencil, savoring the slightly bitter flavor of wood and graphite. After working around sweets all morning, I didn't relish the snacks in the Employees Dining Room. I had the place to myself, except for the new, knock-out EDR cook. Suzanne's cousin was a blonder, bustier, brassier version of Suzanne and had already caused many minor cases of whiplash. She was busy setting up the steam table for lunch. The noisy rattle of the steam table trays soothed me, but the squeak of her soles on the black and white tiles annoyed me, the way a paper cut would, the way this whole damn business did.

CHAPTER TWENTY

I had to give the police credit. They reacted promptly to my tip. The next day, the last day of the year, the homicide detectives returned to the kitchen. The woman wore a London Fog raincoat and Detective Carman wore a black windbreaker. Both were sprinkled with rain. Eldon fluttered around them.

The large female, Detective Peters, stood by her partner with legs apart, her arms crossed over her chest, and her weight rocked back in her solid shoes. The kitchen employees circled the two.

"This is a holiday," Eldon protested. "We're booked by Apple Computers." He stalked the perimeter of the gathering. "We have seven hundred for dinner."

He was more agitated than usual.

"Poison," Detective Peters said.

"Poison?" Eldon echoed.

I noticed she wasn't saying what type of poison. I felt a chill. They probably considered the type of poison one of those niggly details only the murderer would know. I gulped as though trying to swallow a hard-boiled egg. What if the poison had been oleander? What if they figured out that I'd made the call?

Eldon waved a pudgy hand to dismiss the ludicrous idea of poison. "Not in this kitchen."

I was amazed at his innocence. Then I realized it was an act. Eldon knew everything about the restaurant, and we did, indeed, have poison in the kitchen—rodent killer, that we put on the loading dock.

The female partner, Detective Peters, gave me a long, curious look, a full ten seconds of undivided perusal. I stared back, as is my style. She had freckled skin, hazel eyes and short sandy hair. I felt my friends and colleagues regarding me, as the idea of murder settled in. They were taking their cues from this woman, but no doubt some of them were considering my love of murder mysteries and true crime books. I had freely talked about my reference book *Deadly Doses*. Uneasiness surrounded me like a fence. Unfortunately, I could stare down only one person at a time.

As Eldon swished his hand to wave us back to work, Detective Peters raised hers in the gesture for STOP.

In spite of the authoritative signal, Eldon mouthed to Buzz, "The soufflés." Buzz discretely peeled from the group, followed by Ray. Buzz had replaced Fortier and Ray had been promoted from the back line to take Buzz's place.

Detective Peters noticed, but didn't object. After all, they were in sight and could hear from the station. Probably she appreciated a light soufflé as much as anyone. The male detective moved through the circle of bodies, apparently to poke around the kitchen for a cache of poison.

"To get back to your point, Mr. Dunn, we don't think Mr. Fortier intentionally or accidentally ate poison in the kitchen. We're investigating his death as a homicide."

Delores gasped. Those who hadn't already pinned me as a prime suspect glanced around the room as if to spot the maniacal face of a killer. Eldon stopped fidgeting and quieted, as though already composing the most vague possible press release.

"Mr. Fortier had purged his stomach, so the autopsy didn't reveal much besides the poison," Detective Peters said.

"Purged his stomach?" I asked. Terms like "threw up" might not be pretty, but they were a lot clearer than "purged."

"He vomited," Detective Peters said. "In spite of this, the coroner did find traces of honey."

Detective Peters turned her suspicious eyes my way. Again the small mob took its cues from her and a dozen pairs of vigilante eyes targeted me.

This was ridiculous. "Look," I said, "if I'd put poison in my *lebkuchen*, I would have knocked off half our clientele, not just Mr. Fortier."

I had a good idea where and how he'd ingested the poison, but I thought Delores ought to tell them about that.

Detective Peters made another abrupt stop sign and I expected her to say, "*Achtung*!" Instead she droned, "We're not making accusations, Ms.…" She thought a moment about her notes, "…Sabala."

Her fair face went through the mental gyrations I'd seen hundreds of times during my life. She didn't ask the usual, "What nationality is that?" Possibly she'd skipped to the next step of altering her stereotypes to include an auburn-haired, Americanized, blue-green eyed Hispanic, or she'd taken the path of less resistance and decided—erroneously—that Sabala was my married name. Whatever she made of my last name, it didn't seem like a good sign that she remembered it without checking.

"He got a Kris Kringle present," Delores said softly. All eyes turned to her.

"What?" Detective Peters asked.

"He got a Kris Kringle present," Delores repeated.

"What did he get?" Detective Peters demanded.

"Honey."

"Pardon me?"

This was not new information, but the new source of it riveted their attention. "Honey. A little jar with red and white ribbon around it. It looked homemade like *Tio* Victor's." She stopped for a moment as the crowd looked toward her uncle.

Victor shrank.

"I mean, at first, I thought *Tio* Victor must be his Kris Kringle, but now that I know Jean...." She bit her full lips. "...was murdered with the honey, I know it couldn't have been *Tio* Victor."

"Victor had my name," Ray piped in.

The severe hazel eyes of Detective Peters turned to him. "Did he give you any honey?"

Ray gulped. "Well...yeah. But that was a couple of days before Fortier died. It had a blue ribbon on it."

"That's true," Delores said. "*Tio* Victor wouldn't put a red ribbon on nothing."

My wild imagining of Victor as a gang member may not have been so far off the mark. From living in California, I knew the *Norteños* claimed the color and their rival *Sureños* claimed blue. If Victor used blue ribbons and 'wouldn't put a red ribbon on nothing' possibly he did have an affiliation with the *Sureños*. Right now, though, he was white as a gringo.

"Where is the honey, Mr....?"

"Fitzgerald," Ray volunteered. "In my locker."

The male officer, Detective Carman, appeared beside Ray and escorted him toward the locker room.

Everyone waited for more. "And you,...Ms. Medina," Detective Peters said impatiently, "what happened with this red-ribboned honey?"

"Jean ate it with scones. He wanted me to try it."

Esperanza blanched and closed her eyes. "Aiieee."

"Of course I didn't."

"Why not?" Detective Peters asked.

"I'm allergic to honey."

Detective Peters scribbled notes while the rest of us digested this detail. Eldon was shifting from foot to foot and had grown a mustache of perspiration. "Vista Dining Room is sold out tonight," he muttered to the female cop.

I looked over my shoulder. Triumphantly carrying a jar of honey in an evidence bag, her partner returned through the swinging door by the sinks. Ray followed with a sheepish look and mumbled to all of us, "That's been in my locker the whole time."

Even though Ray kept a padlock on his locker, I was appalled the uniforms hadn't found the jar during their initial search. From the grim look on Detective Peters' face, she shared my dismay.

"Detective?" Eldon said, like a boy who desperately needed permission for the restroom.

Peters turned back to him. She was nearly as tall as he, but looked solid, while Eldon looked like an inflated doughboy. "We appreciate the fact you have a busy kitchen to run. We hope to interrupt its operation as little as possible, but we do have a homicide investigation here. Let me make it clear that we have no way of knowing if the poison was administered with the honey."

Her skepticism didn't ring true.

I did suspect the poison had not been administered with the honey in the baggy. At the same time, what were the chances of two jars of homemade honey floating around the kitchen without a connection? I didn't believe in coincidence. Had someone known the poisoned honey might point toward Victor and made the effort to change the ribbon from blue to red?

"We invite all of you to come to the station voluntarily for questioning. We would, at some point, like to talk to all of you, if you know something, or even think you might know something."

The officer smiled sardonically and the mossy eyes looked right at me. "Or, if you're guilty."

CHAPTER TWENTY-ONE

I got lucky. There were twenty-five Medinas in the phone book, but only one Victor and he had his address listed. I slipped on my black sweat pants but paused before I slipped my red hooded sweatshirt from its hanger. The hood would hide my distinctive hair and would be nice if the morning sprinkle turned into rain, but maybe I shouldn't wear red. I decided that I was being paranoid and pulled on the sweatshirt.

My goal was to drive out to Watsonville to see if Victor Medina kept bees at his home, and, maybe, with luck, to talk to someone at the home who was not on high alert. Outside the clouds were already drifting inland. During the drive, I sorted through my logic, trying not to be distracted by the sunshine and the crisp colors of the ocean. The world smelled like fresh soil.

The one person with whom Fortier had tried to share his honey, didn't and wouldn't, sample it. Another coincidence? As far as I knew, the heroines in my murder mystery collection didn't believe in them.

If I assumed Delores's allergy to honey was not a coincidence, where did that leave me? Did Delores kill Fortier, using a food she'd not be expected to taste? That didn't seem likely. It didn't make sense, even if she'd found out about her mom and Fortier. Why would she use a food that called attention to her? Besides, her sorrow was convincing.

On the other hand, what did I know of her acting ability? I'd never been good at dissembling and often failed to recognize it. I hadn't even known my brother was gay until he'd decided to tell me.

Other people might have thought to protect Delores from Fortier, like say, for example, her mom. Eldon had called Esperanza distraught. For all his conversational ineptitude, Eldon made accurate assessments of employees and situations. Maybe Esperanza was distraught. Maybe she had more on her mind than Delores's depression. But, then we had *Tio* Victor, who not only would want to protect Delores, but also who farmed bees.

I turned off Beach Street and followed the numbers down Victor's street. Some of the houses were shabby and peeling, others painstakingly cared for. This was a hopeful neighborhood of upward bound immigrants: homeowners with a nice car here and there, a satellite dish occupying one front lawn, pink flamingos in the rose beds of another. Graffiti blighted fences and sides of buildings in the alleys, but the neighborhood lacked the poverty found across the bridge or in the migrant camps.

Now, in the mid-afternoon, the area was quiet and peaceful. But this was New Year's Eve and by nightfall, some drunken fool would be shooting a gun into the air. Since bullets responded to gravity, Russian roulette would have been a fairer way to celebrate the holiday.

Victor's house was the last on the street before it dead-ended at the levee. It was a white house with two matching squares of shriveled lawn. No car sat in the stubby driveway before the detached garage, and as I parked my Karmann Ghia nobody peeked from the windows.

I slammed the car door, but no one stirred. I kept on my sunglasses and flipped up the hood of my sweatshirt. I rang the doorbell and waited. Nobody answered, but I felt like I was being watched. I glanced at the big window to my left, but the beige curtain didn't stir. I was paranoid.

I scrambled up the river embankment. On top of the levee a concrete bike path followed the curve of the river as far as I could see. A trickle of water flowed through thick brush. From up on this embankment, I had a lovely view of the agricultural land stretching away from the neighborhood toward distant mountains, sharp blue in the fresh air. To my other side, I looked down into the expanse of Victor's backyard.

A little goat ran around in the center of the yard, bleating and bunting at a dodging terrier. *Yard* was a misnomer. It looked like at least a full acre, with a chicken coop and barn at the back. I didn't know exactly what an apiary looked like—some sort of open boxy structure, I presumed. The coop and barn blocked my view into the far corner of the grounds.

A pebbled, concrete patio guarded the weathered back door, flanked on both sides by a riot of plants, both potted and in the ground. No oleander. But Victor wouldn't want his bees to feast on oleander all the time unless he intended to poison everyone who ate his honey. He had given a jar to Ray.

He didn't want to kill Ray, did he?

Although I believed both jars of honey originated here—with Victor Medina—maybe the jar for Fortier had been tampered with later.

As I scanned the yard, my heart pounded with nervousness and excitement. What I was about to do probably constituted stupidity, but I was enjoying the pumped-up, adrenaline rush. I felt sixteen again. I wondered if Fortier experienced the same thrill during his illicit forays into the walk-in cooler. Maybe I was having some sort of early, mid-life crisis of my own.

The six-foot, redwood fence kept the goat and dog from racing off along the river, but it was no deterrent to an able-bodied person. I scrambled down the slope from the levee. I found a knot-hole to use as a toehold and hoisted myself onto the two-by-four top of the fence, grateful for the kitchen work and volleyball that kept my body toned. The little dog looked harmless, but to be certain, I made kissing noises at him. Pink tongue lolling and stubby tail wagging, the terrier bounded toward me.

I dropped into the yard, and a bomb exploded on the back of my head.

CHAPTER TWENTY-TWO

Bugs skittered over my neck and face, but I couldn't move. Something wet, rough and smelly lapped at my cheek.

"*¿Quién es*?" a woman asked.

"Some white chick." The voice sounded young and mystified, but it confirmed what I'd always suspected. Mexicans didn't see anything Mexican in me, either.

The woman demanded, like mothers everywhere, for an explanation. In Spanish she asked why he'd hit me.

"I didn't hit her," the boy retorted defensively in English.

"*¡Dìmelo en español*!" The mother slapped him for not speaking to her in Spanish. Then, before he had a chance to translate for her, she decided she'd understood him well enough. "*Mentiras*," she hissed. The word meant lies.

"I didn't hit her," the young voice whined in English. "I threw the grain bag at her."

I was glad to know I didn't have an army of ants marching

down my neck, just some harmless columns of oats. The terrier whimpered in my ear and licked it.

"*Aiiee, Dios,*" said the long-suffering mother. She picked up my hand with cool, callused fingers and let it drop. I hadn't expected her to let go. My hand plopped into a small, silky pile of grain and came to rest on the rough weave of a gunnysack. I couldn't muster the will to open my eyes. My sunglasses rested on the top of my nose. "*Aeii, mijo, cariño pendejo, ¿porque hiciste esto?*"

While pendejo literally meant a pubic hair, the slang usage translated to something closer to idiot, or dummy. I heard this type of language so often in the kitchen that I understood it even in my groggy state. She'd just asked her dear little dummy why he'd done that.

"She's in red," the boy explained, more respectfully in Spanish. "I thought she was a Northsider. She even has a weird red car."

"*¡Es una gringa!*"

My back had been to him, my hair covered by the hood. "Is she dead?" he asked worriedly.

I waited for the answer, half wondering myself.

"*No sé.*"

A boot nudged my rib cage.

"*¿Que vamos a hacer con el cuerpo?*" The mother asked what they were going to do with my body.

The boy proposed dumping me in the river.

I forced my eyes open. "Abundio." I meant to shout, but nothing came out, so I tried again.

"Abundio?" the boy said to me. "Do you know Abundio?" He dropped to his knees, his freckled face close to mine.

The mom leaned over my face from the other side, another mass of freckles. I squeezed my eyes shut and then opened them again, but Abundio's friendly, goony face was still there. I'd simply died and been reincarnated when he was twelve. "Abundio?"

The two freckled faces gawked at each other and then back at me. The dampness of the ground was soaking through my cotton sweats.

"Emiliano," the boy said.

"*Pendejo*," the mother hissed. She castigated the boy for having given his name. What if the woman filed a police report?

Now that I was awake, the boy argued back in Spanish that I'd been trespassing.

The mother suddenly brightened. "*Mijo, ¿es la novia de Abundio*?" She wanted to know if I could be Abundio's girlfriend.

The boy shrugged and sighed elaborately. "How should I know?" he asked in Spanish.

Spanish shot from the mother's mouth, rapid-fire, machine-gun style, like a Puerto Rican. Children in Mexico did not speak to their parents the way the boy had. This was what happened when you brought your children to "*el norte*." She should send him back to the ranch to live with his grandparents.

Emiliano bent his head, crossed his wrists and looked bored, the tirade as familiar as Mass.

"Ask her," the mother commanded.

"Ah, Mama," the boy pleaded.

She shoved him and we almost kissed. "Are you Abundio's girlfriend?"

I turned my head to empty the grain from my ear and managed to brush my face with a hand. "Yes," I said. "I'm Abundio's girlfriend." This was, no doubt, his mom and brother. For the moment girlfriend status might kindly dispose them towards me. I didn't know how I'd get out of the situation, but it didn't seem wise to underestimate two people who'd calmly discussed dumping my body in the river.

"*Es vieja*," she said to her son.

The boy wrinkled his nose.

I smiled, like I didn't know she'd called me old, and tried to sit up. The mother took my hands and pulled me upright, although I was about eight inches taller and thirty pounds heavier than she was. The wiry, red-haired lady was only a few years my senior. The thought that if my life had been different, I could have a child as old as Abundio, gave me a strange feeling, mostly thankful, but a bit wistful, too. A young woman might be ignorant and inexperienced, but at least she had the energy to raise kids. At the moment, I felt too old for children, or for this kind of escapade. I brushed grain from my sweats and tentatively rolled my head.

"*Venga a la casa por un pan dulce.*" The woman half-closed one green eye and inspected me with a sideways glance from the other.

I used a common defense; I feigned ignorance of the language, and looked, with what I hoped was a convincingly puzzled face, to the boy for a translation.

"Ya wanna have some sweet bread?" he asked.

She nudged her son. They were so similar in size, that they could have worn one another's clothes if he wanted to cross dress in a skirt and blouse, and she in a Giants cap, an oversized, boldly blocked shirt to the knees, and big jeans. She told him to ask my name.

He complained to her in Spanish. He was supposed to meet Freddy. He didn't have time to spend the afternoon translating.

The steely little woman argued back, again threatening to send him back to *el rancho* in Mexico. After a minute of passionate negotiation, they agreed Emiliano would ask my name, and then, he could meet Freddy.

When Emiliano had done his duty, I thought of the Kris Kringle and the little gifts Abundio would have received recently from Suzanne. Then I lied with appalling dexterity, "I'm Suzanne."

The mother grinned with a smile I knew from the kitchen—Abundio's smile. "*Es tan bonita.*"

When I was seated at a Formica table, the mother brought me ice wrapped in a hand towel. I pressed it to my head as she served me *pan dulce* and *horchata*. She pointed at herself and said, "Hortencia."

"Thank you, Hortencia." I lowered the icepack and to be polite nibbled at the sweet bread. I choked down the drink, which tasted like the liquid of rice pudding before it was cooked.

Hortencia remained standing in the center of the worn linoleum, arms folded over her blouse, her eyes squinting at me. "Suzanne," she said meditatively.

I suspected that I would live to rue this day. But since I was here, I needed to make the most of it. I pointed at the *pan dulce*. "Honey?"

Her eyes widened and she grinned. "Sí, sí." She hustled to her cupboards, painted a cheerful yellow. She pulled out a jar of honey and set it on the table. As she watched, I spread a bit on the bread. Mexicans didn't typically eat honey on *pan dulce* and she seemed amused by this *gringa* curiosity.

The jar was half empty so the honey seemed safe to eat. I chewed a mouthful of the bread and made a big show of smacking my lips and making yummy sounds. Life would have been much simpler at the moment if I hadn't pretended not to understand Spanish. Of course, if she thought I could communicate with her, it wouldn't be long before she asked me why I had jumped into the backyard. Thank God Emiliano, her translator, had taken off to meet his buddy.

Hortencia scraped a step stool across the floor and climbed up to reach a top shelf. I stood to see what she was after and felt woozy. But at least for my effort, I glimpsed a shelf stocked with pint jars of honey—all tied with blue ribbons.

She stepped down and thrust a full jar at me. "Very good honey."

There wasn't much left for Hortencia and me to say to one another. In English I thanked her and she understood, nodding and saying, "*De nada.*"

I drove home from Watsonville, feeling foolish. For my rash adventure, I had a throbbing head and a jar of honey. I hadn't learned much that was new. Anyone in the family could access the honey—Abundio, Victor or Esperanza. The Medinas did seem to have some affiliation with the *Sureños* gang. All of Victor's honey was tied with blue, not red, ribbons. And Abundio's mother and little brother had been ready to dump my body in the river, so God only knew what Victor might be capable of.

CHAPTER TWENTY-THREE

The police didn't suspect Victor or Abundio Medina. They didn't suspect Julieanne or Alexis Fortier. They suspected me. I spent the afternoon of New Year's Day in an interview room. I had been summoned.

"Mrs. Sabala…," Detective Carman had said over the phone.

"Ms.," I corrected.

He paused, as though making a note of it, but perhaps just irritated.

"Sabala is my maiden name," I explained. "Only Ms. works with that choice." It occurred to me that Esperanza also used her maiden name—Medina. Victor was her brother. It seemed unusual for a Mexican woman not to take her husband's name and even more unusual not to give a child his name. Could Delores be illegitimate? Esperanza never spoke of a husband or a father.

Detective Carman didn't inquire why I hadn't taken my husband's name, but said, "We'd like you to come down to the police station this afternoon." It wasn't a question, and something about his tone implied if I didn't come to them, they'd come for me.

In a brief fit of paranoia, I wondered if the Medina family had talked to Victor and he had reported yesterday's escapade. One quick description from Hortencia and he would have known I, not Suzanne, had jumped into his yard. I had watched him and Abundio all morning, but they'd acted the same as always. Victor had even told me a couple of jokes.

I'd wanted to ask him directly if he knew I'd "visited" his house, but I'd been overcome by wimpiness. I had a serious bruise on my head, and had been given the third degree by Chad. He'd wanted, reasonably enough, to know where I'd been all afternoon. I'd heard that the best way to lie was to stick close to the truth.

"I went to Watsonville."

"Why?"

"To visit the Medinas."

He'd narrowed his eyes. "I should have listened to Mary."

That had ended civilized discussion and resulted in a sleepless night. Between the argument and my injured head, I had not felt up to confronting Victor this morning.

I reassured myself that this was the SCPD, not the WPD, and that the Medinas were not about to call the police, anyway.

I dressed in a forest green silk blouse. My brother Donald had once told me that was my best color, bringing out the sincere green in my eyes and setting off the auburn in my hair. The color had grown so predominant in my meager wardrobe that I'd invested in dark green pumps. I donned them now below my denim gauchos and inspected myself in the full-length mirror on the bedroom wall.

Good. How could they suspect me? In spite of my bare legs, I looked thoroughly respectable, like a schoolteacher.

I drove cautiously, mindful of road oil loosened and washed up by the recent rains. I tried to calm myself. I had a telephone relationship with Sergeant Gold. He should remember someone as pesky as me. I took Water Street rather than Soquel Avenue to skirt the maze of detours in the downtown. Unlike downtown Watsonville, downtown Santa Cruz retained a bombed-out, war zone look from the 1989 Loma Prieta Earthquake. I found a spot without a meter and pulled to the curb along a yard bordered with oleander bushes, battered white and pink petals sprinkled on the damp ground. The irony appealed to me.

As I crossed the street toward the old police station, my anxiety increased with each step. I stopped by the white masonry, WPA building, part of the beautifully landscaped block of officialdom. A low stone wall separated the rose garden from the sidewalk. "Come on, Carol," I chided myself out loud. *Buck up. This is a real police interview. The inner workings of a station. You love this stuff.* A small, suppressed, sarcastic inner voice said *Sure, in books*. I drew a deep breath, and forced my conservative pumps to move through the dappled shade. I found myself stepping over cracks.

Even the wire mesh on the windows and the faded police department sign didn't mar the beauty of the long, low building. At the end nearest me, an electronic eye circled, watching the entrance and the white and blue cruisers in the lot. The news filmed this building and vandals attacked it, yet, in fact, it housed little of the police department. The building was seriously earthquake damaged, and the heart of the department had moved further up the street to the old telephone company building, an innocuous, ugly, red brick square marked only with a discrete plaque. In spite of my anxiety, I was curious to see the interior. I'd tried to "visit" one day just to see what it was like, only to discover that the front door was locked and one had to speak through an intercom to gain admittance.

"Carol," a voice called out impatiently.

Making a flank attack down Center Street, my nemesis hobbled toward me in her too-tight shoes. "I've been waving for five minutes."

My thoughts were a string of obscenities. What was I going to tell my mother-in-law? She would positively relish the idea that I'd been called to the police department. When she reached me, she clasped a hand to her ample breast. Under her nubby yellow jacket, she wore a ruffled, ivory blouse, equally unflattering, but no doubt, an incredible bargain. "Oh my," she panted, "couldn't you hear me?"

Obviously not. Out loud I managed a civilized, "What's up, Mary?"

"Civic meeting."

Translation: seniors meeting. They usually used the Louden Nelson Center at the other end of the outdoor mall, but with earthquake repair, activities and meetings played musical chairs.

"You're all dolled up," she said.

Why did a basically lazy woman gallop a block down the street to see her hated daughter-in-law? Well, of course, she didn't want to see me; she wanted a ride home. "I can't give you a ride, Mary."

"I don't need a ride." Mary sniffed. "I can call the Lift Line."

A Lift Line named Chad.

"I understand how busy your life is."

I sighed in spite of myself.

"I suppose you have an appointment," she said.

"Actually, I do."

Her eyes flicked around for possibilities, and then with her ungodly instinct, she said, "The police department. I told Chad that you'd get in over your head."

It was my turn to lie. "I'm not in trouble. In fact, I'm going down there to give them a tip."

She stared as though the truth were a pearl in my black, nasty core. Even though I had just lied, I was a basically honest person, who naively expected others to tell the truth. As a basically dishonest person, Mary was suspicious of everyone. She blinked in uncertainty.

But since I *had* given the police a tip, my lie must have sounded convincing.

"Well, then," she said, "I guess I'll just have to sit and wait for the Lift Line."

However, as I continued down Locust, she tagged along, making me nervous. Fortunately, she didn't try to invite herself into the police department.

"Where's the nearest pay phone?"

I shrugged.

"Do you have a quarter?"

This was pure extortion and Mary at her finest. I would have been willing to wager my last ten that if I grabbed her black patent leather purse and shook it upside down, any number of quarters would bounce on the sidewalk. Yet, regardless of the outcome, I'd be the one who'd look, and feel, like an ass. A quarter was a small price to see her backside, but it galled me anyway.

I didn't get a chance to see the bullpen or to find Sergeant Gold and hail him like an old friend. I entered a small utilitarian lobby with offices to the left behind a counter topped with what I imagined to be bulletproof glass up to the ceiling. Microphones seemed to be the only way to communicate with the rabbit warren of workspaces, but Detective Carmen saved me the trouble by striding through the single door. He directed me to an interview room.

He motioned for me to sit. While no bare light bulb dangled from the ceiling, the room was sufficiently austere. It contained a phony wood grain table, three chairs, and metal filing shelves in the corner. Someone hadn't realized the air outside was only damp, not cold, and had turned on the heat. The room felt muggy. I plopped into an upholstered desk chair. Detective Carman sat opposite me in a wooden chair and fiddled with a hand held tape recorder.

"Aren't you going to Mirandize me?" I studied his face and found it handsome, but not as fresh as Chad's or as engaging as Buzz's. It was a face of which I'd tire.

"Let's put it this way," he said. "I invited you to this interview and you came voluntarily. You're here of your own free will and you're also free to leave at any time."

I started to stand, to surprise him.

He gave me a grim half-smile and an abrupt gesture to sit down.

My cheekiness dissolved. I sat back down on the chair.

"After we came to your work yesterday, a witness talked to my partner and told her that you had a book on poisons and that you had talked once about how easy it would be to poison someone."

"Oh, God," I said. That had to have been Patsy. Suzanne would never snitch, but Patsy's first loyalty would be to Detective Peters, a compatriot, a lesbian, although Patsy would use the word queer. Patsy had marched the local Queer Nation through the Capitola Mall, and she took seriously her allegiance to the gay community.

I sucked in a deep breath. "Yes. That is the kind of stuff I like to read. My favorite novel is *Silence of the Lambs* and the niftiest place I've ever visited was the torture museum in the Tower of London. Call me weird, call me odd, call my mom. She'd love the confirmation and commiseration. Furthermore, the book in question was in an unsecured locker where anybody could have read it." In spite of the big breath, my blood pressure rose and the anger gained momentum. "For that matter, anybody could go to a book store and buy that book."

Detective Carman remained quiet. He may have expected a more docile person, but when I lost my temper, I lived up to my mom's often cited, "Fools rush in where angels fear to tread."

I immediately regretted my outburst. I kind of liked Detective Carman, and if I were more extroverted, I might have become a homicide detective rather than a baker with a twisted avocation.

"What about the conversation on how easy it would be to kill someone?" he asked.

"Yeah, we had such a conversation, and I told Patsy poison would be a good way to murder. It's rare, there's no obvious violence, and a homicide investigation often depends upon an aggressive coroner. Don't you agree?"

He gave me a subtle version of the squished-bug look, just a hint of crinkling around the eyes. God, I was beginning to detest that expression. It made me feel like joining Patsy and her radical feminists. If a man discussed poisons or murder, people might consider him knowledgeable or dangerous, but from a woman it was weird and icky. So sue me for not having a squeamish temperament.

"Anonymous tips help," he said.

Sweat trickled down the inside of my silk blouse. Did he know?

"Considering that Patsy was my interested audience for that conversation, I sure hope you call *her* down for questioning." Something about Patsy niggled the back of my mind, but I knew that I wouldn't retrieve it now, under pressure. Whatever the detail was, it would surface, unbidden, when I was taking a tray of hot cookies from the oven or making love with my husband.

"She's been here," Detective Carman said.

"What about Julieanne Fortier?" I persisted.

"What about her?" he asked.

I was indeed getting tired of his face. I read the punched labels under the stacks of forms on the metal shelves: Missing Persons, Substance Abuse Report,.... The cop waited until I looked back. His nose had a bump in it as though it had been broken. Normally, I liked that kind of irregularity, but now it bugged me like a bit of bread dough that bubbled instead of baking into a smooth crust. There wasn't anything I could do about it, but the sight made my fingers itch. I told him the little I knew about Julieanne Fortier.

He explained the term *legitimate suspicion*, apparently what they felt about me.

"Jesus," I exploded. "How many homicides are domestic? Her husband is killed; she's the beneficiary of his life insurance, and she disappears. That's not legitimately suspicious?"

"You know a lot." His tone was flat.

I lifted my hair to give the back of my neck some air.

"There's something familiar about your voice," he added.

"You've talked to me before," I insisted. Shit, if he'd connected me to the tip line, no wonder I was under suspicion. If oleander had been the poison, who would believe that I'd followed a hunch, made a lucky guess, nothing more? I didn't believe in coincidences, so why would the police department?

"What about Victor Medina?" I said desperately.

"What about him?" Detective Carman asked.

CHAPTER TWENTY-FOUR

My mom connected my hot temper to the highlights in my hair. "You got that red hair from my Grandpa Turner," she'd say. He was dead long before my time, but I'd heard a lot about the legendary figure. My mom had shown me a black and white photo of a huge man with a full beard. "His hair was your color," she'd say, "but that beard was red, red, and we're pretty sure he killed Grandma."

"I wonder if I'd have a red beard," I would say, rubbing my cheeks—to annoy her, of course. No body had been found, and I liked to believe Great Grandma Turner had deserted the tyrant, and started a new strain of relatives I didn't know about.

My father's side remained a mystery. He'd abandoned the family before my memory began. My mom, on the rare occasion when she'd refer to him at all, called him "that poor alcoholic man." My brother Donald had looked Latino, but my mom was clearly right about the source of my genes.

I thought about this stuff as I took the freeway to Morrissey

Avenue, and by the time I got home my Great Grandpa Turner's temper had dissipated. Detective Carman was just doing his job.

In front of our house, I stayed in the car for a moment to admire the hardy perennials and large rocks in the front yard and the palm sweeping the cloudy sky. Lola jumped over the redwood fence around the backyard and strutted to greet me, although she looked around in the air to feign indifference.

I climbed from my car. "Hello, my sweet Lola."

She sauntered past and sniffed at a tangle of invasive Mexican primroses. When I opened the door, the aroma of baking salmon hooked Lola's interest. And mine, too.

"Where have you been, honey?" Chad was cheerful, but concerned.

"I don't want you to call me honey anymore," I said.

He looked dejectedly at our two good Willowware plates set out on the tiny table. He had hoped for a romantic evening. He was showered and shaved and wearing a blue and black flannel shirt that I liked.

"I don't mean it like that. It's just that every time I hear the word honey, I think of the murder."

Chad circled the freestanding counter and gave me a bear hug. "Poor, poor, poor, poor, baby," he caterwauled in pity. The flannel was soft and comforting.

I joined the chorus. "Poor, poor, poor, poor, baby." We howled in unison for a full minute and I felt much better.

Chad poured us each a glass of dry Chablis and I related my "interview."

"Carol...."

"Please don't give me a lecture."

Chad set an already prepared green salad on the table and unwrapped Alfaro's four-seed bread that he'd warmed in the oven. He opened his mouth again.

"And please don't say anything about how your mom told you so."

"I won't mention Mary," he said tightly, "if you don't mention Mary."

He dished up plates of salmon and rice. We seated ourselves. "This is as good as anything at Archibald's," I said, "and it doesn't cost twenty-five dollars a plate."

"Fifty, at least," Chad said, "if you count the wine and tip." He relaxed. "I thought the Coho looked really fresh."

Then, when my mouth was fully engaged on a challenging hunk of bread, he said, "Uh, Carol, if there's a link between the honey and the poison, doesn't that mean someone at work killed Fortier? The person who gave him that present?"

I chewed hard and fast, but finally gave up and talked with my mouth full. "It looks that way, but I haven't found anyone yet who drew Fortier's name or who received presents from Fortier. The gift might not have been part of the Kris Kringle. Anyone could have left it for him."

"But wouldn't he be suspicious if he received a gift without being in the exchange?"

"Not Fortier. He had a big ego. He wouldn't have thought twice about a present from a woman, like say Julieanne Fortier, sent into the kitchen via an accomplice."

"Alexis?" he said.

"Well, she is going to inherit her uncle's condo. That's a motive."

Chad shrugged his broad shoulders.

"And why did Julieanne take off after Fortier's death?"

The collar of his shirt lifted the back of his hair as he shrugged again. He was due for a cut. "If she came here to be near Fortier," he speculated, "and now he's dead, why would she stay?"

"Her job."

Chad drained his wine glass. "But what if she thought there would be an investigation, and what if she thought the investigation would expose her role in getting Fortier the program?"

I ruminated on a chunk of bread, and then swallowed. "I'm not sure what her role was in that, but your idea makes sense."

He beamed. Maybe he'd get so involved in the puzzle that he'd stop worrying about me.

"I guess I prefer to believe Julieanne killed Fortier because it's easier than believing one of my friends did it."

CHAPTER TWENTY-FIVE

The next day while on break, I pored over the chart that I'd made on the back of the old recipe. According to the matching I'd done, if Fortier had received the honey from a Kris Kringle, the person had to be Patsy, Big Red or Esperanza. I didn't feel much like visiting the pastry department after my little "invitation" to police headquarters, but I couldn't let that detour my investigation.

I cruised from the EDR, walked along the loading deck, and entered the kitchen by the walk-in refrigerators. The pneumatic seal on the meat door sucked open. Victor pushed out the door and nearly dropped the foam chest he was carrying. He stood in a puff of cold air.

The whole scene struck me as odd. "What were you doing in there?"

Victor set down the ice chest, turned his back to me and padlocked the door. "Buzz sent me to get a roast. This seemed like the best way to carry it."

Buzz wasn't supposed to give anyone the key. Maybe that's why Victor seemed stealthy.

"Don't worry. Your secret is safe with me," I said.

I got as far as the garde manger before I lost my resolve to confront Patsy.

Suzanne saw me hovering there and sang out, "Haven't seen much of you."

"Busy, busy, busy."

"Trying to figure out which one of us is a killer," she retorted with good humor. She clapped a hand over her mouth and grimaced. Peeling carrots, Delores hunched over the sink.

"I'm amazed we don't have a machine to do that," I said.

Delores smiled weakly at me.

Suzanne's slim hand wielded a knife the size of a small machete. She pressed a row of bright, exposed carrots to a cutting board with the heel of her hand, the fingers curled. At the rate Suzanne chopped, her fingers could be added to the salad before she even knew they were missing.

"Eldon more or less implied I should back off," I whispered.

"Oh, God. Eldon," she moaned. "What am I going to do, Carol?"

I'd been so preoccupied with my snooping, I'd lost touch with other events in the kitchen. I knew only what any fool could observe. Eldon would let Suzanne's breaks stretch to twenty-five minutes, and never roust her from the EDR. If he looked at his watch when he was near Suzanne, he did so to avert his eyes. He never approached her. She never had to listen to him. And she most certainly had never been written up. It was easy for her to like him.

"I don't like him like that," she protested.

"Like what?"

"God, Carol, you have been out of it. Don't you know about the stuff he gave me for Christmas?"

"Let's go for a beer sometime soon, Suzanne."

"Eldon's only half of it," Suzanne whispered. "Abundio's been acting so weird toward me."

I gulped. "I've gotta hustle. My fifteen minutes are up. Eldon's already been on my case this week."

I felt like a student saved by the bell. Eventually, though, I'd have to tell Suzanne about how I'd used her name. I should probably do that before the mom Hortencia let drop some physical detail about their visitor.

As I flew up to the pastry department, Patsy gave me a tight, non-smile. I glared at her and suppressed the first-grader instinct to call her a tattletale.

It struck me as one of life's mind teases that she and Esperanza were the toughest women I knew, yet they fussed over spongy petit fours and gooey meringue shells.

"Esperanza," I called.

The woman turned from a tiered cake. She had the same flaring cheekbones, full lips and slender nose as Delores, but her eyes were brown. Her face hardened when she saw me. She held a paper sleeve full of icing, and baby blue frosting smudged her smock.

"Yes?" she asked.

"Have you had your second break?"

She shook her head.

"Come visit me, okay?"

Waiting for Esperanza, I wiped down the stainless steel counter for the third time. No second shift replaced me. The last part of my work would be easy, organizational tasks. I was the bakery, except for whatever poor fool got stuck in my slot on Friday and Saturday mornings. This week, though, I'd been scheduled for six days in a row. Eldon managed to do that without paying overtime by making sure the sixth day fell into the next pay period. He was sneaky like that.

Esperanza turned the corner, drying her hands on a small, white terry towel. "Sorry, I had to finish a cake. Dose people," she said with her thick accent, "dey have a reception here today."

Esperanza was only a few years older than I was but seemed of another generation. Perhaps parenthood caused the shift. Maybe one day I'd be seventy-six and still relate to teenagers better than to grandmothers. Perhaps the difference was cultural. She had the dignity of an indigenous person mixed with the toughness of a field worker and the style-consciousness of a women's magazine reader, her eyelids painted mauve to plum, her cheeks brushed with matching blusher.

"I just have one question," I lied—I had about a hundred. "Whose name did you draw for the Kris Kringle?"

She frowned. Although her hands surely had to be dry, she kept wiping them. "I drew Todd for the Kris Kringle." She waited. I didn't want her to leave, but I couldn't formulate a relevant question about Todd. He was a young, curly-haired, back-line cook with no apparent motive to kill Fortier, even if he, like every young guy in the restaurant, had a crush on Delores.

"Thank you for the nice presents, Carol," she said.

"I saw you put one of those glow-in-the-dark Band-Aids on Delores."

She nodded. "I am worried for Delores. She's so heart-broken."

"You're a good mother."

Tears sprang to the corners of her eyes. This woman did not crumble easily. Eldon was right. Esperanza was distraught.

"Come on," I said. "Let's get out of this place." I laid my hand on her stiff shoulder.

As we walked by Victor and Abundio, she pitched the towel into a blue, plastic milk crate. Victor spoke tersely to her in rapid Spanish. As they no doubt intended, I didn't understand much—only *inmigración* and the tone. It warned.

I didn't get a clue about the murder, at least not any that jumped up and bit me, but I did learn about Esperanza. She and Juan Rocha had grown up in Gomez-Farias, a small town near Zamora, Mexico. Many of the villagers, migrant workers who picked crops, traveled between Mexico and the Pajaro and Salinas valleys.

After her *quinciñera*, her fifteenth birthday, Esperanza married Juan. The families had known each other and Juan and Esperanza had grown up together. Their families wanted them to marry and fortunately they were fond of one another.

In the first two years of marriage, Esperanza gave birth to Guadalupe and Juan. When Esperanza was seventeen, they packed two plastic bags full of supplies, left the children with Juan's mother, and used their savings to ride a bus to Tijuana. In the evening, they walked the brown, barren hills along the border to La Colonia Libertad.

"Dere were a hundred people, jus' waiting for night, so dey

could run down the hill. All we had to do was climb a fence and dere was MacDonald's and all the tings of America."

We sat in the EDR. Esperanza munched apple coffee cake, several days old. "How do you stay so skinny when you bake so delicious food?"

I smiled. "I could ask you the same question." She'd borne three children, but a person would never know it. Her body was sinewy, her stomach flat, her breasts large and firm.

"Wedding cakes are not delicious." The smooth face relaxed as the brown eyes turned inward, thoughtful, as though considering the metaphoric implications of the statement. "We had tortillas, and water, but I was so scared I could not eat a tortilla. Helicopters flew over, so low dey make dust turn 'round. I was sure we would get caught.

"Someone tol' us to drow away the plastic bags because dey were white. Juan wrapped our tings in a spare shirt. Someone said to forget dem. We need to run.

"When it got dark, people moved. We did, too. When the spotlight came over, we would drow our bodies on the floor or in the bushes. Then some horses came right toward us. Juan went in the bushes but a man on a horse shined a flashlight in my eyes. Dey handcuffed me and took me in a full bus to a deportation camp, like a prison, with wire fence all 'round. I had a hearing and dey sent me back to Tijuana. A lot of people walked back to the hills to try again. I didn't know what to do. Juan had our money. I had no way to go back to Gomez-Farias, so I walked up to the hills.

"Dat night I got across okay. I begged money and lucky I got an operator who could speak e-Spanish. I called Victor. He told me where to go and what to do until he could get me. I never saw Juan again."

Esperanza's story plagued me for the rest of my shift. At first, the search for Juan had detained her in Watsonville.

After a couple of months, Victor had suggested, "Maybe the *cabron* took a hike."

"No. *No es posible*."

"If we find him able to come, but not here, I'll cut off his *cajones*."

Across the cafeteria table, the tough little woman had smiled at me. "You understan'?"

I nodded. "If Juan deserted you, Victor would have killed him."

"Yes," she said, without hesitation. "Yes, he would."

Victor had planted doubt in Esperanza's head. In Mexico, her life with Juan had existed in a carefully crafted vessel, hard as adobe, earthy as patted tortillas, slow as a *paseo*. But once they had scrambled over the fence and Juan's boots thudded on American soil, the vessel and its dreams shattered. Everything was different in America.

As months passed, Esperanza thought maybe Victor could be right. She stopped looking. Run down and weak, she collapsed in an artichoke field. Victor took her to a clinic that diagnosed hepatitis B. After the long illness, poverty chained her to the fields of the Central Coast.

When she had finally returned to Gomez-Farias, with money

for a coyote to smuggle her children, they did not recognize her. Like Chad, little Guadalupe and Juan had come to know their grandma as Mama. They had cried and clung to her at the mere idea that the stranger might take them, and, in the end, Esperanza had returned to the United States alone and broken-hearted.

"You see, Carol, I am not a good mother."

It was the same conclusion I'd reached about Chad's mom, but given Esperanza's circumstances, her self-judgment seemed harsh. Maybe if I knew more about Mary, my judgment of her would seem harsh, too. I gritted my teeth and resolved to be more understanding with the woman.

Her "*hija natural*," Delores, had been born four years after Juan disappeared.

Esperanza's story made me think Victor, to honor his sister and to protect his niece, might have killed Fortier. The honey, after all, connected him to the crime even if the jar did have a red ribbon on it. I yawned. It was a theory, no better or worse than my theory about Julieanne.

CHAPTER TWENTY-SIX

By the time I finished work, I felt emotionally drained. I'd barely shut the door of my Ghia, when a black Harley roared up beside my parked car.

Patsy was decked out in black leather and a law-abiding helmet. She motioned for me to roll down the window.

I didn't mouth, "Fuck off," through the glass, although I was tempted. But rather I complied, locking her eyes in my steeliest stare. I noted with satisfaction that the motorcycle, now stopped, presented a challenge for her straddled legs.

"I just want you to know that I didn't go to the police to tell on you."

"Oh?" I asked.

"There was some other stuff I thought Sasha should know."

"Sasha?" I asked, with an obnoxious, insinuating flutter of lashes.

"Detective Peters," she clarified, struggling with her black beast. "And just for your information, Carol, she's not gay."

I hated knowing that I'd jumped to a wrong conclusion.

The Harley turned a little this way, and then a little that way. "I didn't want Sasha to find out through the investigation about Fortier and me."

"You and Fortier!" I exclaimed in a most impolitic way.

She pulled back her shoulders, offended. "Why not? I have great tits." She sounded sarcastic and angry.

I half expected her to rip open the black leather jacket to prove the merit of her breasts. Perhaps she would have if the motorcycle had been less demanding. Something was going on here that I didn't understand.

"You and Fortier had an affair?" I asked.

She rolled her eyes. "Hardly."

I felt dense for at least the tenth time since I'd gotten involved in this mess. I didn't even know what question to ask.

"Fortier saw me as the ultimate challenge," she said. "He was one of those guys who believes a woman could only be a lesbian because she hasn't met the right man. Namely him."

"He raped you?" I guessed.

She considered the question. "No one but me would think of it that way."

"Jesus, Patsy." I remembered her bitterness last summer in the sports bar. Yet, I'd never heard a peep about this in the kitchen. Below its surface of dirty jokes and juicy gossip, I glimpsed a black reservoir of secrets. "How was Detective Peters going to find out about this if no one knew?"

"Did I say no one knew?" She fired up the machine and roared off, leaving me to wonder whether she'd simply finished all she had to say, or I'd pissed her off, or she'd gotten tired of fighting the weight of the Harley.

As I watched her vroom down the hill and into the trees, I realized if Fortier had participated in the Kris Kringle, his name had fallen either to Big Red—or to Patsy.

At home, I fixed myself a stout cup of coffee and parked myself on our brick landing. I needed to figure out what to do next. Lola circled in the Peruvian lilies, preparing to lie down. She squashed a section of the flowers into a nest. "Get in there and lay some eggs," I told her.

She curled in the long, slender leaves and squeezed her round eyes shut with either annoyance or pleasure.

I sipped my black coffee and processed the new information from Patsy. If Fortier had raped her, Patsy had the perfect motivation to murder him. She would have considered the deed environmental cleanup.

I reached out and absently petted Lola's tail. She gave me one sharp meow and a scathing look.

Patsy hadn't wanted Detectives Peters and Carman to stumble onto her secret. Better to tell them, especially when she had a sympathetic audience like Detective Peters. She might not be gay, but Patsy had called her Sasha. They must know each other.

Patsy had suggested someone else knew about whatever had happened with Fortier, someone who had kept his or her mouth shut, but who might now talk.

The flower is pure Patsy. The niggly detail that I couldn't remember at the police station popped into my head. The petit four that Eldon had said was specifically for Alexis had been decorated by Patsy, but I'd eaten the damned thing instead. I doubted Patsy had shared that tidbit of information with Sasha.

The memory of spewing over the balcony made me gag. I looked at the contented, brindled ball of fluff in the crushed flowers. "Come on, Lola," I urged. "If the Easter bunny can lay eggs, so can you."

CHAPTER TWENTY-SEVEN

Mist dampened my face. Like fingers reading Braille, my feet followed the bumps of the path from the employees' parking lot to the kitchen. The night was moonless and the stars shrouded in fog. Sometimes the night cleaning staff were around—distant vacuums smothered in fog pillows. This morning I heard nothing—no noisy cart rattling along the sidewalk. In the still, dead air, the eucalyptus leaves didn't rustle. Even my footsteps were muffled.

No light spread itself into the wet air—no late revelers, no early risers, no pacing insomniacs. Three-thirty may have been an obscene time to go to work, but it was a lovely to walk in the deep quiet through a seamless velvet. I savored the solitude, the sense of floating as though through outer space.

I walked to the far side of the building and ascended the steps onto the loading dock, screened from the bricked horseshoe of the main entrance by an island of artful landscaping. The door was locked, but I had my keys in hand, as I always did in the dark. For all my love of the stillness, I was a realist. I didn't carry a purse and I practiced a wary look.

I entered the building, turned to the poorly lit time clock, and punched in. The brightness of the locker room blinded me. The lights should not have been on. I felt myself tense, even though occasionally someone did arrive before me, or someone forgot to turn the lights off.

I zipped through a rack of clean uniforms, arranged by size, smocks on one side, pants on the other. I ignored the divisions, and looked for the smock with the prohibited "Carol" on the inside of the collar in indelible black. After I found my top, I began pulling out the pockets of pants to find the one with my name on it. I'd marked one of the hound's-tooth checked pants when I'd finally found a uniform that fit. I had a fastidious dislike, anyway, of wearing other people's clothes, laundered or not.

I couldn't shake the creepy feeling that someone was around. My ears felt as though they were rotating back, like an alert cat's, listening for unfamiliar sounds.

I sat on the bench in front of the lockers, and stripped off my sweats. The one time I'd seen Fortier in his birthday suit, he had been sitting right here, doing what I was doing, except he apparently didn't bother with underwear.

I'd debated a sexual harassment report. I hardly needed to tell anyone, though. Fortier had crowed about the situation with special exaggeration of my expression.

Young guys like Todd and Ray were amused. Buzz looked like he'd rip Fortier's head off. Eldon ignored him. Patsy snarled, under her breath, "Fuck with my fluff, and I'll bite your balls off," to which Fortier responded, "Try it, you'll like it." Typical kitchen banter. But maybe the police would see her remark differently, the way they chose to view my remarks.

I slipped on my uniform. Some people put locks on their lockers, but I operated on the assumption that people were about as interested in my ancient, stained sweats as I was in their clothing. I was fortunate enough to have a top locker and right now the only thing in it was a pair of sturdy, steel-toed, flour-encrusted shoes.

I plopped my sweats and high tops in the locker. When I pulled out the work shoes, a paper fell to the tile. I opened the sheet of typing paper folded into fourths, and found letters cut from a newspaper. The form struck me as a comic anachronism, like a ransom note from a re-run of Perry Mason. The letters jumped around on the page like they must for a dyslexic. They said: STOP SNOOPING. IT WILL HURT PEOPLE YOU LIKE.

I froze. The message was ominous. Until that moment, emotionally, I hadn't believed the murderer walked among us. Now, it was no longer an intellectual exercise. What did it mean about my hurting people I liked? Was this a threat of more violence to come? Or was this the murderer letting me know that he—or she—was dear to me?

Had someone just delivered it? Was that why the lights were on? I flung open the locker room door.

As I stepped into the dimly lit hallway, the note's message was driven home. A figure stepped from the EDR and clobbered me on the head.

CHAPTER TWENTY-EIGHT

The person who hit me needed a remedial thug course. The blow hurt and stunned me, but it didn't even knock me down. I suppose it did the job, though. As I grabbed the side of my face, shook my head to clear it, and opened my mouth to scream, a door slammed and footsteps pounded along the loading dock.

I wasn't about to chase someone through folds of clouded night. Especially not in my stockinged feet.

I opened and closed my mouth a few times to see if it worked. I had the impression I'd been struck with a flashlight, although the idea didn't make sense. The attacker had been too far away. The person had apparently intended to hit me on the back of the head, but a squeak had alerted me and I'd turned into the weapon. The object caught me on the jaw, cheek, and upper lip. The lip throbbed. I ran my tongue along it, but didn't taste any blood.

Stuffing the note into my pocket, I walked shakily up the hall to the women's room and inspected myself in the mirror over the sink. The lip was swelling and the skin under my cheekbone was tender to the touch. I'd probably have a bruise there. I peeled up the lip. The inside looked like an overripe plum. It would be a while before I kissed Chad.

Indignation blotted out the pain. I could understand why someone would murder Fortier, but why would someone from the kitchen slug me? Neither of the blows to my head had been serious, but if my life continued this way, I could end up like Muhammad Ali.

I crossed down the hall to the EDR, and for once in my adult life, wished my mom were around. Not so she could comfort me, but so she could educate my assailant.

"You can't beat any sense into her," my mom would say, shaking her grayed head. "She's too perverse. She's been like that since the day she was born." Her short, unpainted nails would pick at her knitting. "Why, she wouldn't come out, even when Dr. Kremetz induced labor. Two days later, she changed her mind and didn't even give us time to get into the delivery room...."

I scooped slushy ice from the salad bar trough, wrapped it in a white terry towel, and pressed the compress to my lip. I returned to the locker room to put on my work clogs, which waited patiently for me on the bench as though nothing had happened.

As I made my way up the hall and through the kitchen, I flicked on more lights. I managed to unlock the first refrigerator while still holding ice to my lip. I hated the nuisance of the padlock and wondered, as I entered the cold, how much good it had done in preventing theft. I had access to Eldon's key. Buzz had a key. Buzz sent Victor to fetch stuff.

The cluttered disarray of the Use-First shelf had invaded my space again. A half dozen new items surrounded the original offending half jar of olives. I had to set down my bucket of coconut macaroon dough and my ice pack to relock the door. I clumsily made my way back to the bakery. I hefted and banged the pail onto my table, wrung the wet towel into the dishwashers' sink, and set the white terry ball on my stainless steel table for future use. Facing the entrance so no one could sneak up on me again, I scooped mounds onto a tray. They looked like heads and I fought the urge to smash them in revenge.

I fantasized that I had pursued my attacker, tackled him, punched him in the face, hog-tied him with my kitchen smock and called the police.

Gradually I calmed and thought logically. Who could I trust? Not anyone in the kitchen. The less I said, the better chance I'd have of staying a step ahead of the killer. I wanted the person to be unsure and nervous, to make a mistake. I would make him—or her—think I harbored other suspicions.

In the stillness, through my noises and the hum of electric appliances, the door by the refrigerators clicked shut. My heart raced.

I breathed deeply. My internal clock said others should be arriving. Still, I pulled my rolling pin from the wire racks. Hugging the hallway, I peeked into the kitchen.

The person whistled *I Saw Mama Kissing Santa Claus.* I relaxed. Buzz.

I stepped into the open as he rounded the corner by the refrigerator.

He smiled and walked behind the back line toward me. He reached out his arms.

I jumped back.

"Carol?" he said, arching his pale eyebrows. "What's wrong?"

My mind and heart warred. My heart wanted to let him enfold me while I blurted the whole nasty affair into the warm turn of his neck. My mind said out loud, "What are you doing here so early?"

Annoyance flashed in his blue eyes. "It's not that early, Carol." He dropped his hands melodramatically, as though I'd smacked them down. "What are you doing wielding a rolling pin and sporting a fat lip?" He mimicked my suspicious tone.

"I'm rolling dough."

"You are not." He heaved a big sigh that smelled like vanilla. "You're making coconut macaroons."

"Then none of your business."

"If you say so." He wheeled.

"Well," I said to his back, "you didn't answer my question."

He looked back, the always accessible Buzz.

"Why you're here early?"

"I'm here early because Ray hasn't mastered lead line." He waited, expecting tit for tat.

"I tripped in the dark."

"And fell on your lip." He nodded and strode across the kitchen.

Buzz turned on his steamer. He whistled again but it sounded like a funeral march.

I was beginning to relax when Victor leaped around the corner and asked, "Do you know why the pervert crossed the road?"

He smiled in anticipation, combing his black hair with one hand. Then he squinted and stretched his bulky neck to get a better look at my face. His brown skin flushed and he touched his own lip involuntarily, asking the question with his fingers.

"I fell," I explained.

The hand returned to his hair and I noticed the freshly skinned knuckle. The kind of injury a person might get from hitting someone. Maybe Victor wasn't a clown; maybe he was one fine actor.

"Why did the pervert cross the road?" I asked, amazed at the calmness of my voice.

"He was still attached to the chicken."

He saw my eyes on his knuckles. "I hit something this morning," he said.

Not *something*, I thought angrily. *Me.*

When Suzanne dropped by, she didn't waste any time. She walked right up to me and said, "Oh my God, your lip."

"I fell." It sounded lamer every time, like abusive mothers who claimed their maimed children *fell.* If I kept this up, someone might think I was covering for Chad.

"You iced it?" She picked up the wet towel, and checked its cleanliness. Her face wrinkled in disapproval to find the bunched cloth empty of cubes. "I'm going to get you more ice."

She strutted off toward the outside icemaker and returned with a bulging, clicking bundle, which she thrust toward me.

I obliged and held the cold pack to my lip. It felt good.

"I was going to ask if you wanted to go for that beer today," she said.

"It's only a fat lip," I said. "When do you wanna go?"

"How about when I get off?"

"Fine. I'll just hang out and have lunch here."

She peeked around the corner and then ducked back into my bakery.

"What's up?" I asked her.

She sighed. "Abundio's there now," she whispered. "I don't know why, but he suddenly seems to think I'm fascinated with him."

She saved me from trying to muster a response by dashing off.

As I worked, I mulled over the case. Something about my snooping had upset the killer. Could it have been my visit to Victor's house? Then why had he waited until today? It didn't seem like my questions about the Kringling should worry anyone, even if Fortier had participated and Big Red or Patsy had drawn his name. It was about time I completed that chart, but it wouldn't prove anything. Even if I established who might have given him the honey as a present, another person in the kitchen could have doctored it. Besides, why would anyone use a gift traceable to him or herself as a murder weapon? But then again, death row had no shortage of stupid people.

I sighed. I needed more little grey cells.

At lunch, I asked Alexis for Julieanne's phone number in New Orleans. Let the killer think I was going back to my original, corny idea that the wife did it.

Alexis was smashing peas for the pleasure of smashing. She

barely met my eyes. I had the feeling she would never forgive me for seeing how vulnerable she was.

"Oh, Julieanne decided to come back," she said.

CHAPTER TWENTY-NINE

When Suzanne finished her shift, she and I returned to the sports bar where she, Patsy and I had been in the summer. The bartender remembered Suzanne. "Did you come back to watch that cooking show?" he kidded.

Suzanne's eyes widened. "That man, the Cruz'n Cuisine King, is dead."

"Oh." The young man looked crestfallen, not at the news, but at his *faux pas*. "I owe you a drink," he said to Suzanne.

Suzanne shook her head. "I'm not getting a beer. I want something expensive. A brandy Alexander."

He took her no as a no, and I decided I liked him, even though he had no neck and didn't know I existed. I'd absorbed enough of my mom's Puritanical nature to consider hard liquor in the afternoon decadent. I ordered a Corona with lime.

We waited for our drinks and then went to the table farthest from the counter. In order to forestall the subject of my lip, I launched into an account of Chad's jealousy of Buzz, and how I'd grown unsure of Buzz's intentions lately.

"Don't worry." Suzanne patted my hand. "Buzz is too smart to be that stupid." She pulled off her hair ribbon and slipped it around her wrist. "That didn't sound right. I mean he knows you and Chad are tight." She shot me her wide-eyed look. "Everything is okay with you guys, isn't it? I mean I did notice that you didn't bring Chad to the party."

"Oh yeah, we're fine." I didn't sound convincing, but it didn't matter. Suzanne looked distracted.

"Speaking of tight," she blushed and looked around, "I've been worried about Buzz," she whispered.

"Huh?" I leaned across the table. "Has he been hitting on you?" I tasted jealousy, like a rotten nut.

"He might be blurring boundaries. He's fallen off the wagon."

I sat stunned, letting the whispered words coalesce into meaning.

Suzanne's hands fluttered in frustration. "I don't mean he'd have to be drunk to come on to you." The nervous hands toyed with her drink glass. She hadn't yet taken a sip. "God, nothing I'm saying is coming out right."

"I didn't take any offense," I assured her. "But why do you think Buzz is drinking?" I tried to sip my Corona, but my fat lip sucked into the opening. It stung. I broke down and poured my beer into the glass. "He has a MADD bumper sticker on his car, for Christ's sake."

Suzanne bit her lip.

"You think Buzz is so insincere? That he'd plaster a message on his car that he doesn't mean?"

Suzanne reached across the table and patted my hand. "I can tell you didn't have any alcoholics in your family."

"Don't condescend to me," I snapped.

Suzanne jerked away her hand.

"Sorry," I mumbled. Apologizing was not my forte. The guy who gave me the name Sabala, hardly a dad by anyone's standards, had been an alcoholic, but I had no memory of him, so it didn't seem worth mentioning. "I guess you've had some experience?"

"My dad. Believe me, sincerity doesn't have anything to do with it." She snapped her wrist with her scrunchie. "An alcoholic can look you in the eye and say that he won't drink again, and the next day be falling down drunk. And you know what? He was sincere when he said it."

Even though Buzz had confessed his DUI to me, I realized that I had come to the conclusion that I wanted, that it had been a one-time lapse.

Suzanne snapped her wrist to a stinging pink. "With an alcoholic, others are always to blame." The punitive finger she'd used to snap herself wiped condensation from her glass like a windshield wiper. "Remember the Christmas party?"

I nodded.

"Buzz smelled like rum."

"Like eggnog," I said.

"Rum," she insisted. "I saw him drinking the kitchen sherry, Carol." She blushed.

I felt ill. Granted that our kitchen used only the finest sherry, not cooking sherry, the action retained the desperate quality of Kitty Dukakis drinking fingernail polish remover. "What did you say?"

"I didn't say anything. I was too embarrassed."

"Does Buzz know that you saw him?"

"I don't think so."

I sighed and looked around the bar—dark wood, lots of beer and sports advertisements, and no ferns. Patsy, Suzanne, and my glib plotting of murder seemed a lifetime ago. At this time of day, the bar was cool and dim. A friend of the bartender sat at the counter and they argued amiably about the Buffalo Bills. Occasionally, the bartender let his gaze slip over to Suzanne.

I thought of Buzz's vanilla breath, and I realized why people use expressions like *heartache* and *heavy heart*. Sorrow swelled in my chest until it felt cramped.

"What are we going to do?" Suzanne asked.

I shook my head. "I dunno."

She let silence reign for a while and sipped her drink. "Should I change the subject?" she asked, recapturing some of the Suzanne lightness.

I nodded.

She reviewed the presents Eldon had given her as her Kris Kringle. Some of the things like the truffle and teddy bear had been within reason, but he'd also given her opal earrings and a cashmere sweater.

I remembered Eldon in the mall the night of my own frenzied mission. While I'd never call Suzanne greedy or materialistic, she liked nice things that with our pay she couldn't afford. "Sit back and reap the rewards," I suggested.

"But I feel guilty."

"Why should you feel guilty if a guy chooses to dote on you?

Has Eldon asked you out?"

"Good God, no!"

"Then, what's the problem?"

"I feel like I'm leading him on."

"You're just being gracious. How would he feel if you gave the presents back?"

She snapped her slender wrist with the pale blue band again. "I know that would be humiliating. And if I embarrassed him like that, what would happen to my job?" She collapsed on to her arms, folded on the heavy, dark wood of the table, and rolled her eyes up at me. "Oh, God, Carol. What should I do?" She seemed about sixteen.

I didn't feel like a person to give advice. If a problem involved just one's self, I could decide on a course of action that felt right. But throw in another person, and problems became complicated. I did think Suzanne was over-reacting a little. "I told you. Relax and enjoy the bennies of having the boss wrapped around your pinky. For all you know, he doesn't want anything but a Platonic relationship."

She straightened. "Now I know you're not taking me seriously. When's the last time you met a guy who gave you a hundred buck's worth of stuff and only wanted to be friends?"

"He could be different."

Suzanne yanked the band from her wrist and screwed her angel-food-cake face into an expression resembling a withering look. "Eldon is different." She jerked up her hair until she looked like a troll doll and ensnared the curls in the blue band.

She had me there. She sipped her brandy Alexander and licked froth from her pink lips. "Do you think this is sexual harassment?"

"As sexy as your lips are, I don't feel harassed when you lick them."

She rolled her eyes.

I thought about her question. "I don't know. You don't like Eldon's attention, but he gave you the gifts as part of a Kris Kringle. You don't have any case if you haven't let him know his gifts made you uncomfortable. And even then, he'd have to keep giving you stuff for it to be sexual harassment."

"Catch 22," she said. "If I tell him, then he might fire me."

"If he does, you have a case."

"Who wants a case?" she moaned.

We sat quietly for a while, trying to see a creative way out of the circle. "Well," I said, "there is the possibility he'll take rejection like a man."

"That's what I'm afraid of."

We laughed.

"Did you know the police came back to Archibald's yesterday?" Suzanne sensed what people did or did not want to discuss, and asked the question tentatively, testing the waters.

"No, I didn't." I'd been so busy dodging queries about my lip, that I'd again lost track of the bigger picture. I tried my beer, but it tasted flat and warm in a glass. "What did they want?"

"It was weird. They went around asking all the same questions you did."

"Like what?"

"You know. Who drew what person and like that. That's why I started worrying again about the presents Eldon gave me."

I felt both proud and annoyed that the detectives were following my routine. "Do you know who Patsy and Big Red drew?"

She shrugged. "I don't know who Patsy had, but Big Red had Buzz."

I thought about the chart I'd made. If I weren't mistaken, this tidbit left only one conclusion. "Do you know if the police matched everyone with his Kris Kringle?" I tried to keep my voice nonchalant, while my body vibrated from a surge of adrenaline.

"You, for one, were already gone, although I suppose someone knew who you had. Who did you have, anyway?" She drained her glass. The bartender hustled over.

"Want another?"

He didn't check with me, but then, I had a half glass of stale beer in front of me.

"No, thank you," she beamed at him. "I have a pleasant buzz."

The word buzz made her face fall, and I felt mine follow suit.

The bartender shifted uncomfortably, probably wondering what gaffe he'd committed now. "Would you like some pretzels?"

"No, thanks. How about you, Carol?"

The bartender looked at me, his eyes taking in the lip, and then moving back up.

I felt like screaming, "I'm not a battered woman!" but realized I was. I had been hit, and by someone I knew. "No, thanks," I mumbled.

He left.

"That's one thing about having gone with an older man," Suzanne said, trying to cheer me up. "It moves the whole game of seduction to another level."

To hear something positive about a relationship with Fortier disappointed me.

She glanced toward the bartender. “Young guys are so obvious.”

And Fortier wasn't?

An arm covered in blue mohair whipped impatiently through the air. “So easy.”

“Eldon's older,” I teased.

CHAPTER THIRTY

Soquel Drive followed along the outskirts of Live Oak before descending to the white, steepled church, the picturesque centerpiece to Soquel Village. I told myself that I was taking this route to avoid the rush hour on the freeway, but I also wanted to delay this necessary and overdue confrontation.

I hoped that Patsy's partner wasn't home. Ana, aka the Bulldog, was immense, not big and muscular, but a woman for whom the adjective obese was invented, fat to the point that seats on planes and busses became issues. Ana's body was the center of her universe and she had a one-item political agenda. Granted work needed to be done in the area of women's body images, but even those who agreed with her found her intimidating.

I turned right off Soquel Drive and headed toward the ocean. I made a left by a small string of shops, salivating at the sight of Manuel's Restaurant. I hadn't eaten since after work when I was waiting for Suzanne. Even with the car windows up, I could smell the Mexican food through the salty sea air.

A quick right brought me to Ana and Patsy's spruced up beach house. Real estate agents would call it a "doll house," a pale blue-gray charmer with white shutters and white picket fence. Their front lawn was exceptionally green, the flower borders manicured although nothing was in bloom. Smoke curled from the chimney. I felt bad about disturbing this domestic tranquility.

Patsy opened the door before I knocked. She was dressed completely in black: thick black socks, black jeans, black sweater pulled over a black turtleneck and her ears dotted with onyx studs, throwing her shock of mauve hair into high relief.

"I didn't know whether you or the police would figure it out first, but I've been expecting a visit."

She gestured me into the living room. The fireplace screen was open and the andirons lay on the hearth, the only items out of place in the room. Ana wasn't on either of the sturdy couches and Patsy looked so pale that my nervousness dissipated.

Aware that this wasn't a social visit, she didn't offer me anything to drink.

"Your lip is sure swollen," she said, as she perched on the brick hearth and poked at a log. "I guess you know that I drew Fortier's name." She kept her gaze on the fire. Her voice sounded matter of fact.

I sat on the edge of one of the blue and white striped couches. "You know, until I completed the chart, I didn't believe he participated."

"You never talked to Ray."

"That's true. But if I remember right he had Delores's name."

Patsy turned. The fire was blazing, but she didn't shut the screen or put up the poker. "Fortier tried to finagle her name from him."

I thought about Eldon trading for Suzanne's name and wondered if there was any point of having a drawing in the first place if everyone was going to swap names to get who he or she wanted. Had Buzz traded to get my name? I blushed at the thought. "Obviously Ray wouldn't switch."

Patsy smiled. "Yeah, that was cool. Ray's had a crush on Delores since her first day. The only reason Fortier participated was so he could get Delores's name. He wanted to give her a vibrator."

"So why didn't you tell me or the police this?"

"Why? So you'd think I gave him the honey?"

"Did you?"

"What I don't understand, Carol, is why you care who killed him. The person did the world a favor."

"I guess it has to do with truth, justice and the American way," I said lightly, so she could take it as a joke if she wanted. "So, did you kill him?"

"No." She turned and gave the log a vicious poke. It tumbled from its stand into the corner of the fireplace, shooting up embers. Patsy jumped. "Fuck!"

The agitated woman lifted the poker. I hopped up from the couch. Not again, I thought. I did not want to get hit twice in one day.

My imagination was in overdrive. Patsy put the poker in its stand and picked up the tongs. She busied herself with maneuvering the log back into place.

"If you didn't give him the honey, what did you give him, Patsy?"

She laughed bitterly and twisted around to look at me. "At the time I thought it was funny. But in retrospect, I can see it was just mean spirited. Like the syrup of ipecac that I put in that petit four."

I deduced that one person had known about Fortier and Patsy and that had been Alexis. But Patsy was right about the mean spiritedness. I got really sick from that petit four. Even if Alexis had blindly sided with her uncle, even if she'd lorded her uncle's power over Patsy, she didn't deserve the treatment I'd received. The girl was hardly more than a teenager. She was entitled to a degree of misplaced loyalty and obnoxious behavior. They were survival techniques until she could become more of an adult.

Remorse softened Patsy's strong face. "I was as bad as Fortier. That's part of the reason I didn't want anyone to know. I didn't give the son-of-a-bitch anything."

CHAPTER THIRTY-ONE

Kicking wrinkles from the extension, I dragged my home phone from the bedroom and sat it on our small table. I made a second trip for the phone book.

I plopped on the wooden chair and watched Lola through the sliding glass door. She hunched, peering through the dusk at movement under the lantana. I turned to the yellow pages and found a beekeeper supply store in San Jose. It wasn't quite 5:30. Even if they'd already closed, someone might be there to answer the phone. I dialed.

A pleasant, older-sounding woman answered.

"I was wondering if you could tell me how far bees travel for food?"

"They'll travel a long ways, sometimes miles, to forage. That's why, if a beekeeper wants to label his product clover honey, clover has to be the primary foliage for a two-mile radius."

"Thank you," I said. "I think that answers my question."

It seemed unlikely that Victor, or anyone, could control bees enough to produce a reliably poisonous product. That would involve a painstaking effort. A long-term, obsessive plot. Fortier's murder didn't have that feel.

But Victor was still the guy with an apiary and he hated Fortier. He was the one with the scraped knuckles after my attack. On the other hand, would a guilty person flaunt incriminating evidence? He could have worn a bandage and said he had a cut or burn, such a common occurrence in the kitchen that no one would have thought twice.

Lola sprang into the bush.

I tried to think of a good story to explain my lip to Chad. If I told him the truth, he'd be worried about my safety, when there wasn't much danger. If the person had wanted to kill me, he could have easily done so. I believed the person, at most, wanted to scare me. Or, the person may have just delivered the note and been interrupted, hitting me out of fear.

I thought about once when I'd wrenched a weed from the ground. It turned out not to be a weed at all, but a shoot from a tree. I'd strained with all my might until the growth snapped and my hands, clutching a long, green strand of leaves, flew back and blackened my eye. I could tell Chad something like that.

Later I told him the whole truth and nothing but the truth. He took a pack of Camels from his beat-up Levi's jacket and shook one out right in front of me.

"Chad!"

He opened the glass door, stepped out onto the bricks, struck a match and lit the cigarette. Dusky, cold air rushed into the house.

"If you don't want me to smoke, don't tell me shit like this."

"Well, I considered lying."

"That's not what I mean."

"What you mean is I can be held accountable for your smoking. That pisses me off."

Chad turned around and exhaled smoke in a thin, angry jet. "Don't be such a hypocrite, Carol. If you don't want me to endanger my life, why should I let you endanger yours?"

"My life is not endangered," I said.

He licked his fingers, pinched out the cigarette, and put the unsmoked portion back in the pack. "Who's in denial here?"

"You're twisting everything, Chad."

He stalked into the kitchen, not at all calmed by the nicotine. "Then let me make my meaning clear. Tomorrow I want you to go down to the police station. I want you to report what happened. And, I want you to stop poking around in this murder before you really get hurt."

"Are you telling me what to do?"

"Am I stupid?" He managed a faint smile. "I am merely, for once in my life, Carol, telling you what *I* want."

CHAPTER THIRTY-TWO

Chad was long gone when I opened my eyes. He liked working in the winter. In spite of the increased danger from dampness, the roofs were cooler and work was limited by the shortened daylight. By nature, he was a laid back guy.

My mother had made the patchwork quilt resting on top of me. I contemplated it lazily and thought if one wanted to get literary, it might symbolize our relationship. All manner of sizes and shapes had been hastily machine sewn with no discernible pattern and the corners puckered. My mom had inherited more of her Grandpa Turner's impatience than she'd ever admit. Yet, the quilt had so clearly been made for me with deep, forest green and dusty rose the predominant colors, a little gold for dazzle, and a ruddy brown to stabilize the menagerie. Inside my mom had inserted an old blanket to give the quilt weight and warmth. The backing was a durable but soft flannel.

It was ugly and I'd never buy it, but if the house caught fire,

I'd dash through flames to rescue it.

I stretched one foot, then the other, feeling the cramped bow of my arches. I touched my rubbery lip and wondered if collagen produced the same weird, stretched smooth texture. If it did, how did models deal with having their lips feel like beach balls?

Lola padded up from the foot of the bed and meowed in my face.

"Oh, poor Lola," I whimpered. "Neglected and starving."

I closed my eyes.

Lola reached out a paw, unsheathed one claw, and poked my hand with it.

"No!"

She sprang from the bed, walked indignantly to the living room, and scratched the couch.

I leapt out of bed. "Stop that, Lola!"

She fled under the table. She had me up. Now she just had to get the hand to reach under the cupboard, grab a fistful of IAMS, and throw the crunchy nuggets into the bowl.

She peeked around the table leg, widened her green eyes, and meowed once, as piteously as possible.

I refused to be manipulated by a cat. I held up a spray bottle full of water. "See this, Lola?"

She shrank behind the leg of the table.

"I'm going back to bed and I'm taking this with me."

I stomped to the bedroom, set the bottle on the stand, and hopped back into the delicious warmth.

I did not look forward to humbling myself to crooked-nose Carman. I considered Chad's request reasonable, but I didn't want to do it. This was the kind of situation where marriage got tricky.

Lola hopped on the bed, sauntered up my body to my chest, and peered into my face.

I snaked one hand into the cold and scratched her spotted ear. "Such faith in my goodness and restraint."

She purred, circled, crushed a boob, lay, and began to bathe.

My pleasures were simple. I loved lying in a warm bed with a happy cat on my belly.

I wrangled with my conscience and reached this compromise. I'd go to the Police Department, but I wouldn't make an appointment. If no one could see me, too bad. I could look Chad in the eyes, throw up my hands, and protest, "I tried."

I had the weekend off, a rare opportunity, and I planned to take advantage of it, maybe see what Julieanne Fortier was up to these days.

Chad's request that I stop investigating had to return to the bargaining table. I'd tell him that I understood his concern, but there were things I had to do to be me, dangerous or not. If he argued, I'd remind him of my support for his bungee jumping escapade, a seventy-dollar expense for a completely nonsensical, one-minute thrill.

He'd claim it wasn't dangerous.

Simultaneously, I searched my brain for a retort and planned a visit to Alexis and Julieanne.

Julieanne and Alexis Fortier lived off Capitola Road in an apartment development, four boxy buildings that heaved, brown and stark from a field, the parking lots fresh, tarry insults to nature, the landscaping recovering from shock. Ten years ago the Live Oak area of Santa Cruz had narrow roads through spacious lots, grazing pastures, and large vegetable gardens. Now the sometimes tastefully designed, but always cheaply constructed, monstrosities erupted everywhere and cast long shadows over the original bungalows and farmhouses.

Alexis and Julieanne lived in the back building, facing a creek. I climbed concrete and metal steps, the freestanding kind that reverberate, to a small concrete landing with an orange door to my right and to my left.

I rang the bell for the door on my left. When it opened, a miasma of smells wafted from the room like oily heat waves from a busy highway. The palpable stench surrounded Julieanne, who wore a dirty, blue knee-length terry robe. Curlers dangled from her hair. I didn't know anyone still used them.

Exhaling cigarette breath, she scowled, making uglier the tear-soaked, alcohol-bloated face. "I don't want any."

"I'm a friend of Jean's," I lied before she could close the door.

She narrowed her eyes.

"A co-worker," I amended.

"Oh, yeah," she said. "I remember you from the funeral." She backed up a step and yanked curlers from her hair. "Wanna come in?"

That was grounds for philosophical debate.

Julieanne had the house closed up, all shades and curtains drawn. As my eyes made out my surroundings, the swampy smell separated into its components: whiskey, Kool cigarettes, the toxic odor of the new nubby, dark blue carpet, and the pizza box and coffee grounds in the overflowing garbage can at the end of a counter. This sloppiness didn't go with my impression of compact and spry Alexis, but I had no problem pinning it on Julieanne, now slouched and spreading on the couch. Against the backdrop of muted stripes of color, Julieanne picked at her eyes' crusties, and then combed her hair with the hand.

I sat away from her, on a wooden stool pulled up to the kitchen counter. Without any embarrassment, the woman poked through a heap of elbows in the ashtray, straightened the most promising, and lit the crooked third of a cigarette.

"Rough time," I said ambiguously.

"Jean's death unhinged me," she stated, quite matter-of-factly for an unhinged person.

"Why did you return to Santa Cruz?"

She exhaled, a leisurely and sensual act. "When I got back to New Orleans, it heightened the fact Jean was gone. That's where we courted and married. His family likes me, and they've never recognized the separation. Good Catholics." She bent the butt of the finished cigarette—her trademark. "But here in Santa Cruz, Jean never belonged to me. Not really. He never needed to divorce me. I let him have whatever he wanted."

For a moment I thought she'd cry, but she finished strongly. "Anyway, I got to New Orleans and said, 'What am I doing here? I don't have a job. I like Santa Cruz better and Alexis is like a daughter to me.'"

More like a mother, I thought. "Do you have a job here now?" I asked.

"Well, no." She seemed surprised by my question, pulled her robe more securely around her and peered at the mound of butts.

"I guess you quit your job at KRUZ TV?"

Her mind, numbed by alcohol, tears, and self-pity, slowly sensed I had not come to offer condolences. "That's right."

"Why?"

Suddenly she didn't care about her hair or whether the robe pulled apart to reveal ample cleavage. She stalked past me to the kitchen, poured herself a half glass of Jack Daniels, straight, and took a gulp. She coughed. "Who are you?" she asked in a strangled voice.

"Carol Sabala."

She coughed several more times, pounded her chest, and then slugged down some more as though that might help. Tears sprang to her eyes now, but they weren't from grief. "I mean who are you?"

I sank into a metaphysical quandary, unable to speak. Where did one start—a baker, a thirty-three-year-old....

I avoided the imponderable by resuming my offensive. "Did you quit because of the mess Fortier got you into? Were you afraid the murder investigation would reveal how you and Fortier screwed Buzz Fraser?"

"Jean Alcee didn't get me into any mess," she snarled. She slammed the glass onto the counter and slung her arms across her formidable chest.

"Do you mean it was your idea?"

"No," she said. "What I mean is I'd happily do anything for Jean."

There were two options. She was lying. Or, she meant it. I'd met people like that who wouldn't take responsibility for living, but stuck to others like cockleburs and rode through life on the blind side of a leg. These people scared me.

"Did you kill him?" I asked.

She looked mystified. "Jean didn't want to die."

CHAPTER THIRTY-THREE

No matter how snotty I got, Detective Carman maintained a professionalism designed to incite madness.

I cursed my bad luck—that he'd been there, that he'd been eager to see me, and that I was back in the humid room. My underarms steamed crescent moons into my gray turtleneck.

I'd dutifully reported the whole episode of the fat lip, resenting every minute of it.

He'd suggested that I back off and let the police do their work, to which I'd made a snotty comment about their progress.

He ignored it. "Not because we're afraid you'll undermine our investigation," he said, "but for your safety."

"You don't think ordinary citizens can solve crimes?"

He sighed and pushed the report form across the table, indicating with his index finger where I should sign.

"You have nice hands for a policeman."

"We're saying this for your protection," he said. "We have no doubts about your ability to scare the perpetrator. After all, he assaulted you."

"So what you doubt is my ability to protect myself?"

He refused to be baited. A long finger capped with a neatly, manicured nail, tapped the paper. "Let's put it this way. If I were you, I wouldn't eat anything at work."

Even though sweating under my heavy hair, my neck prickled at Carman's words. "You said 'he.' Do you think my assailant was a man?"

Carman sat sphinxlike, waiting for my signature.

"A friend of mine said you returned to Archibald's and asked about the Kris Kringle. Do you think it's important?"

He leaned back in his chair. He shook his head.

"No?" I probed.

"That shake means you're impossible."

"My mom would agree. But, if I were a man, you'd both call me determined."

He glanced at the unsigned report and wiped his forehead with his shirt cuff. His dark hair looked damp at the tips. Since he was obviously hot, I wondered if the room was overheated on purpose. "To be honest, we don't have the time or energy to pursue an obstruction of justice case."

"Obstructing justice? Me?"

He rubbed his chin. "If you withhold information."

"All I have are theories, and I tried to share those with you before."

"You mean the Julieanne Fortier idea?"

"That was one."

"Was?"

"I went to see Julieanne Fortier today and eliminated that possibility," I confessed.

"Eliminated? How?"

"Julieanne would have blown Fortier's brains out if he had asked her, but I sincerely doubt he requested her to put oleander in his honey, so I don't think she did it."

"Oh," he said, with a twitch of a smile, "solid evidence."

I looked down as though reading the report and a trickle of sweat rolled to the front of my neck.

"We could view that as tipping off a suspect."

"Alexis is my co-worker. I have a right to visit her if I want."

"Alexis is at work," he said.

My instinct—about which he was so skeptical—registered with the sensitivity of a lover's lip the promptness of his reply and the timbre of his voice. "You keep awfully good track of the people in this case."

His hesitance was the kiss of certainty.

"So you and Alexis...." I fluttered my fingers and smirked. I could picture them together. Although Alexis was petite and Carman average-sized, they both had compact bodies, large brown eyes, and humped noses, Alexis' by nature and Carman's most likely by a fist. They'd age into lookalikes. I could imagine them wearing matching shirts and walking hand in hand at the mall. "Fortier left Alexis a nice condo," I teased. "Maybe the two of you plotted the whole thing."

"I met Alexis on this case," he said. "I haven't asked her out. I won't until the case is concluded."

He was so forthright that I felt ashamed of my prying. I certainly didn't want to discourage him. Alexis needed someone to distract her from her hopeless crush on Buzz. "Can't we work together?"

"My question exactly."

We sat across from each other locked in a childish staredown. I'd honed the skill with my mother and it came back to me in an instant.

He blinked first. "What do you want?"

"If you tell me one thing, I'll sign this and then we can both get out of this steam bath."

"That's extortion."

"And I'm a bitch. But if I were a man, this would be negotiating and I'd be called tough."

Carman didn't agree or disagree to the deal.

"Did you ever find the honey?" I asked.

He snorted. "That's your question?"

I nodded.

He seemed relieved. "No. We didn't."

CHAPTER THIRTY-FOUR

On my second day off, housework became unavoidable. As I pushed our oiled dust mop around the oak floors, my mind meandered through motives.

Buzz had the best one. Revenge for stealing the show. If Fortier had discovered Buzz was drinking again, maybe he had used that against him in other ways as well. Fortier's death had not only eliminated any future threats, but also positioned Buzz for a move into management, not that Buzz would have any interest in management. He wasn't that concerned about money. He liked to cook. Revenge, pure and simple, would be his motive.

Dust balls and cat hair collected before the gray ropes of the mop. I swept through a column of ants, marching toward Lola's bowl. I pushed the mess onto the piece of cardboard Chad and I kept behind the refrigerator. It worked better than our dustpan.

I dotted a terry-cloth rag, part of my last bathrobe, with lemon oil, and started the most boring, and therefore the most neglected task—dusting. After the first windowsill, my dust cloth was black, but I didn't fold it yet, as the others were just as grimy.

A whole chain of people had advanced because of Fortier's death, but that didn't seem like a strong motive since we all received abysmally low wages.

Until the day before yesterday, I'd never considered Suzanne a spurned lover. She might have been more jealous of Delores than any of us dreamed. The truth was I found revenge and ambition better motives because I understood them better. Jealousy mystified me. I'd long ago decided if a person didn't like me, that was his problem, and if he liked someone else better, that was his prerogative. Competing for a man's affections was a waste of energy.

Another possibility was money. Maybe Alexis had killed him for the condo. I wondered what Carman thought. He hadn't asked her out yet. That could be out of professionalism, as he claimed, rather than any real suspicion.

Now that I'd finished windowsills, I folded the cloth to a fresh spot for the furniture and realized I should have started with the cleanest stuff first. That showed how little expertise I had at housework. I felt equally as inept with my investigation.

I kicked myself for wasting time on the Kris Kringle. Even with all the givers and recipients matched, anyone could have slipped Fortier the honey, including Alexis. Since Patsy, Fortier's Kris Kringle, had opted not to give him anything, Fortier's only curiosity about the honey was probably why he had received just one present.

I hated to throw away a good rag, but every fold was now black with grime. I filled a gallon jug with Miracle Gro and water and made the rounds of my neglected plants.

There was the possibility of a jealous Delores. The police had never found the jar of honey. Maybe Delores had fabricated it. A distraction. No, Eldon had corroborated its existence. Well, how about the protective uncle, who not only raised bees but had scratches on his hand, or a protective mother….

I needed to find out more about Esperanza's *hija natural.* A weird thought tapped at my mind. What if Fortier had had his fling with Esperanza nineteen or twenty years ago? I tried to dismiss it. Certainly he'd know if he'd gotten Esperanza pregnant. I couldn't believe Fortier would make a play for his own daughter. Yet, I knew such ugliness existed.

The phone rang. "Hello." Silence greeted me and I guessed at the caller. "Mary?"

"Isn't Chad there?"

"He had a job this morning."

"Oh, I thought he'd be home."

Fat chance.

"Well, would you please deliver this message to him?" the long-suffering voice began. "Tell him that I had to go to the Social Security office because they're saying I've been using the wrong number…."

The woman would have needed to moan to sound more self-pitying. I felt fury bubbling up in me. This woman had abandoned her baby, left him with her parents. Granted she had divorced her alcoholic husband and already had a twelve-year-old boy to support, but it's not as though she'd settled down to that task. Instead she'd tried on men like suits of clothes, until finally after about ten years she remarried to a man who turned out to be worse than her first.

"…and then after I do that, I'm going to have to ride the bus all the way out to Emeline…."

"Mary, I don't know when I'm going to see him."

"But you will tell him, won't you, that…."

I seethed. What claim did Mary have to Chad's devotion? After marrying her second jerk, she had retaken custody of Chad who was already eleven years old. They had no control over the older boy Ashley, a grown hoodlum. He did nothing. When they tired of his sponging, Ashley stole what he needed. He resented his younger brother. Chad, on the other hand, longed for his grandparents. Only when Ashley beat him, blackened both eyes, broke his left arm, cracked a rib, and left contusions up and down his legs, only when Chad was taken to the hospital and Child Protective Services got involved, only then did he get to return to his grandparents.

The stuff Mary griped about constituted the mainstay of her life, but she talked as though she were being singled out and intentionally harassed. I stifled the urge to tell her these were her problems. I could refuse to tell Chad, but he would not appreciate it. And that's what I hated most of all. In spite of her neglect and irresponsibility, he loved her.

"I'll tell him." I sounded as martyred as she did. Chad would, however, get an edited version. I was not about to guilt trip him for her.

After the call, I sat on the back steps and did some serious thinking about murder. To be more honest, I pictured Mary and me in the kitchen. I had a frying pan in hand. Mary pushed my buttons, the Turner temper blazed, and KAPOW. The scene didn't even strain my imagination.

But the crime at Archibald's had not been done in a fury. It had been planned. I imagined collecting some oleander. Easy enough. There was a bush of it at the corner of our street. I could see myself boiling it into a syrup and mixing the potent poison in some honey, but I couldn't see myself actually giving it to Mary. Whoever had killed Fortier must have really hated him.

CHAPTER THIRTY-FIVE

Chad unlaced and pulled off his boots. His body sank deeper and deeper into the couch. He reached for the remote.

Later I would casually say, "Oh, by the way, Mary called." If I told him now, he'd jump up to return the call. For the moment, I wanted him to relax. And to be mine.

Chad flicked through the channels, stopping on the local news. Unlike me, he didn't mind if someone talked while he watched television. He didn't become engrossed; often he had to switch back and forth between programs to generate enough interest and action to hold his attention.

"Chad," I said in my most buttery voice. I curled beside him and put a hand on his thigh.

His head whipped around. He eyed me suspiciously. He expected me to confess that I had not really visited the police yesterday. He couldn't believe that I'd done what he wanted, and he knew me too well to think that I had complied fully.

I held his hand and met his eyes. I'd mastered my technique by age ten. His face changed like a composite sketch as information was added. The eyes mottled with hurt, worry, and guilt. In spite of his concern, he loved me too much to force me to change. I wondered if this meant he loved me more than I loved him, since I had no intention of stopping my no-smoking campaign.

Chad gave me a chagrined smile. "So, what's up?"

"A new angle."

He sighed deeply, but didn't protest. He had already known there would be one, and accepted it. He flicked through the channels.

Hungry for a trustworthy audience, I spewed my latest idea about Fortier and Esperanza—that Delores could be their offspring.

"You think Fortier is sleeping with his own daughter?" His incredulous, grossed-out voice churned up all my doubt. "Why? To get revenge on Esperanza? Someone who dumped him twenty years ago?"

"Not really," I said lamely. I pushed to the other side of the couch to pout. "But then, I don't think anyone would sleep with his daughter, but guys do."

"Well, Delores isn't Fortier's daughter."

"How do you know?"

Chad's tight lips, hurt eyes, and flurry of channel surfing reminded me that he was barely tolerating this.

"You're forgetting high school biology."

He sounded condescending.

"Enlighten me."

I sounded sarcastic.

"Delores is a blue-eyed *babe*."

For all my pontificating about jealousy, ice-cold needles stabbed my heart. Usually Chad couldn't keep my co-workers straight, much less remember the colors of their eyes.

"Esperanza's Mexican and Fortier's French, right?" he continued.

"Both brown-eyed," I said, letting his argument sink in. It *was* highly unlikely that Delores was Fortier's daughter. Yet the Medina clan clearly carried around genes for fair hair and skin. Esperanza's relatives had red hair and freckles. But I didn't want to argue about biology and recessive genes. My mind was mulling over Chad's words. He didn't call women *babes*.

CHAPTER THIRTY-SIX

On a small square of waxed paper in the center of the stainless steel bakery table, creamy caramel rolled down from the white stick plunged into an apple's heart. Around the stick, the rich brown had thinned to reveal a circle of green, most likely a crisp Granny Smith. The caramel, collected on the waxed square, beckoned to my finger. While I didn't feel like eating a whole caramel apple for breakfast, I could scarcely resist a sample.

But Detective Carman's words haunted me: "I wouldn't eat anything at work." Scarier still, the person who'd put the apple on the table knew me well, knew that working in the bakery, I was immune to the temptations of cookies, muffins and pastries. However, I loved the tart and sweet crunch of a caramel apple. If I left it around, it would lure me all day.

I pulled out the two-foot rolling pin and whacked the apple as though it were a rat. I didn't want to be tempted to fish it out of the newly lined garbage can. Shaken, I wiped up the smashed bits of apple and shook them into the fresh plastic liner. I threw the towel into the wash, cleaned and stashed the rolling pin, and lathered my hands with soap. I fought tears. This whole thing was getting to me. I was not cut out to be a detective.

I collected my wits and headed to the cooler for my dough. I heard a whistled rendition of *Jingle Bell Rock*.

I wanted to bolt to the phone in the hall, to call Chad, and to keep him talking for the next hour until someone else got to work. I didn't want to be alone with anybody in the kitchen. My stubborn, stupid streak rooted me as the whistling grew louder and louder.

Buzz came out of the back hallway and beamed at me.

"Christmas is over!" I snapped.

He stopped whistling. He stopped walking. He sat down the tray he'd been balancing on the prongs of a hand.

"Carol?" he said softly from across the room. "Tell me what's wrong."

"That apple. You left me that apple."

"Yes," he said. "I thought you loved caramel apples."

"Why?"

Like a pubescent boy, he looked down. He wore steel-toed work shoes. From across the kitchen, I could see the blush crawl up his fair neck. "I like you."

"You can't like me," I stammered. "I'm married." I moved my arms like an adamant umpire calling safe. "Forget it."

"I respect that, Carol," he said so quietly I barely heard him. "It doesn't stop how I feel."

I felt stupid to my toes. My eyes stung with frustration. I had possibly made an egregious error and humiliated my favorite person in the kitchen. "Why'd you give me that apple?"

We stayed frozen on opposite sides of the kitchen. Since I'd already asked Buzz that question, he pondered alternate responses.

"I gave you the apple to make up after the other day. I felt bad that I'd pushed you to tell me about your lip. That's the kind of thing a person has to be ready to talk about."

"Chad didn't hit me," I blurted.

"I didn't think he did," Buzz said, too quickly.

Perhaps he had thought Chad and I were on the fritz. What better time to make a move? Or perhaps he'd killed Fortier and had now given me a special treat injected with arsenic. Perhaps he was drinking again, and had lost a firm grip on reality. Perhaps, he was the kind, gentle soul I'd always thought, trying hard to cheer up a friend who'd been behaving in a strange way.

This scene sucked, but at least I knew what I had to do.

CHAPTER THIRTY-SEVEN

Without getting my dough, I turned back to the bakery. I snatched the dirty towel from the wash and pinched smashed apple from the clean, garbage can liner.

I felt his presence behind me and whirled. Buzz blocked the doorway.

My heart hammered.

He stared at the apple fragments in the white terry.

"New recipe?" He flashed a sardonic smile and lifted one blond brow.

"Cobbled apple." The riposte came from some altered state while my conscious mind scrambled to decide whether Buzz Fraser meant to kill me. If he drank our kitchen sherry on the sly, and apparently he did, I didn't know him, and I didn't know what he was capable of, except masterful deception. Behind me lay the rolling pin. Just a couple of steps and an arm's reach.

"You are acting bizarre." Buzz stepped into the room. "Are you afraid of me, Carol?"

I nodded. Buzz was not dumb. My fingers trembled as they folded the towel around my evidence. Forensics could confirm or assuage my doubts.

"You think I killed Fortier?"

I decided if he weren't guilty, nothing would happen if I reached for the rolling pin, and if he were guilty, I needed an equalizer. I bounded and stretched. So did Buzz.

As I jerked down the rolling pin, he caught my wrist, but I continued the momentum with my whole body. The wooden roller slammed into his thigh with reassuring solidity.

"Jesus Christ, Carol!" He did not loosen the manacle on my wrist. "I knew you were going to do that!"

I kicked at his shins, but he jumped back, his grip on my wrist plunging me forward. I heaved around my left and hit him on the side of the face hard enough to hurt my fist.

"Let go of the goddamn rolling pin, Carol!"

He grabbed for my free hand, but I hopped back and kicked at him.

He stuck a foot behind my leg, tripped me, and caught me as I fell. He stumbled after me on to the floor, sprawled over my body, and pinned me to the tile. He panted. His chef's hat had fallen off and his fine hair puffed in various directions.

I bucked and twisted.

"Stop it, Carol."

"You stop."

"I will when I know you don't intend to hurt me."

"Me hurt you?" I said angrily, thinking about ways to inflict great bodily damage.

"You don't think I'd hurt you? Do you?" he asked. He searched my eyes. "I didn't kill Fortier, Carol. And I'd never, ever hurt you."

"You're hurting me now."

He released my arms. I could have bashed his head with the rolling pin, but I'd decided he was telling the truth.

"Why did you follow me in here?"

His hand reached for my hair. I jerked away.

"Because I couldn't stand having you shut me out." The large fingers caressed my cheek, gently stroked my hair. "I've cared about you for years, Carol. But it seems like ever since Christmas, ever since you figured it out, you've felt compelled to treat me like shit."

"I thought you poisoned that apple to kill me."

Buzz shook his head. Straddling my lap, he reached up to the table and pulled down the white terry package. He opened the towel and stuffed bits of apple into his mouth.

I panicked. "No! No! Spit it out, Buzz! Spit it out!"

For some reason he did as I commanded. He secreted his mouthful into the towel as delicately as an Archibald's customer disposing of an olive pit. His gaze roamed over my face. He spread over me, my body sandwiched between cool ceramic and warm muscle. I thought a thousand things, but my lips had a mind of their own.

It was the saddest kiss of my life. Beyond the tender lips and the breath mint, I could taste it, the fumes rising to his mouth from the high-octane pool in his stomach.

CHAPTER THIRTY-EIGHT

"What are you doing?" Victor said.

Buzz and I untangled and stood. Victor didn't wait for an answer to what we were doing. He rolled his eyes and beat a retreat to the storage room. Usually Victor moved stealthily. After he left us, he made sure everything rattled and jingled and thumped as he loaded stacks of plates and heavy rubber honeycombs of cups and glasses onto a cart.

Buzz and I stared at each other. I felt flushed. He was an excellent kisser. I brushed bits of grit from the forearms of his smock. He dusted my back. "How's your face?" I asked.

"Your kisses would fix anything."

I percolated inside. I loved this man dearly, with enough lust to kindle a fire.

"My thigh still hurts," he suggested.

I shoved him. "We need cold showers."

"Together?" he asked.

I shook my head.

Buzz reached down for his hat and put it on. I picked up the towel and my blunt instrument.

"You've been drinking, Buzz."

He shook his head in perfect denial, but where was the surprise, the shock at my statement?

"I haven't had a thing, Carol."

My body throbbed, charged with the kisses, but I was too single-minded for an affair. I lacked any refined skill at duplicity. I also loved Chad and any hint of disloyalty from me would bump his occasional insecurity into permanent paranoia.

"You haven't had a thing this morning," I qualified.

Victor clattered by with his cart. He looked studiously forward.

Buzz lightly clasped both my hands. "I don't regret our moment," he said, "and I'm going to make damn sure you never do either, Carol."

He kissed my forehead.

I grabbed him and hugged him with all my might. "Suzanne saw you drinking the kitchen sherry," I murmured.

His body stiffened in my grasp. "Big Red gave that to me as a Kringle present. He didn't know about me," Buzz said miserably. "He wanted me to try it."

The lie was elaborate. "Buzz, when you kissed me, I tasted alcohol."

He pulled away. His blue eyes looked shattered, like marbles baked in an oven. Shaking his head, he backed into the kitchen.

CHAPTER THIRTY-NINE

When Victor pushed by with his empty cart, I called to him.

He jumped. "Ay, *a la chingada*," he muttered. "I didn't see nothing."

"It's not that," I said. I waved him into the bakery.

"First Buzz, now me," he teased.

"I thought you didn't see anything."

He smiled sheepishly. He gaped at the towel on my table.

"You're here early," I said.

He continued to stare at the towel, his strong face contorting at the sight of the smashed apple. "Is that *cabron* kid. He's home sick."

"What's the matter with Abundio?"

"Cold, flu, his hair, his freckles, his *como se dice*." He pointed a stubby finger at the terry cloth. "Wha's that, looks like baby caca?"

"That's some apple that Buzz spit out."

He shrugged as if to say *gringos* were past figuring.

Fair enough since I couldn't figure myself. Why had I screamed for Buzz to spit out the apple?

"I bet they screw me and don't get nobody to help me," Victor griped. "Do you wanna bet a dollar they screw me, Carol?" He thrust out a hand for a wager.

The masticated apple on the towel distracted me. Obviously, even as Buzz stuck the apple in his mouth, I'd thought it might be poisoned. Did I believe Buzz had poisoned it, and then enacted an elaborate charade? I was going nuts. I shook my head.

"Don't wanna bet, huh? Smart lady. They'll screw me."

Did I think someone had spotted the apple during the brief interval it'd sat there, had dashed off for some poison and a convenient syringe, and then had rushed back to inject the apple, without being noticed? *Ludicrous.* I didn't know how I could persuade Carman to test it. I carefully folded up the mess and sat it on the wire rack shelf. Detective Carman deserved to receive it. He had planted the idea that the murderer might try to poison me.

Victor's dark eyes watched as though the world had gone mad and he was helpless in the face of it.

"Victor, you know that honey Fortier received?"

"You mean that honey that made me a suspect. Course I don't know nothin' about it." He half turned and looked toward the cart in the hall. He wanted to leave, but, in spite of his rough edges, Victor had been raised as a *caballero*, a gentleman. He wouldn't turn his back as a lady spoke to him.

"Was it some of yours?"

"Carol, I think it was. But I didn't give it to him."

"Didn't it have a red ribbon on it?"

"Yeah, sure." He shrugged. "Anybody could change the ribbon. I seen the jar. Jus' the kind I use."

"You saw it! Did you tell the cops?"

He gave me an exasperated look. I remembered his fears when the police had arrived. He was an illegal. The last thing he wanted was to interact with the police.

He forgave my stupidity and added, "When Fortier got that present, Abundio came back and *me dijo*, 'Sheck it out.' I couldn't believe it."

"Did other people have access to your honey?"

"Oh, sure. It's my usual present. Jar to Suzanne for her birthday. Abundio, of course. We live in the same house. I gave some to Esperanza and Delores. And one jar to the *jefe*."

"Eldon?"

Victor squirmed.

"Eldon?" I prodded, more gently.

Victor tugged an earlobe and kept his eyes averted. "Well, he hired my whole family," he said defensively.

CHAPTER FORTY

The rain drummed and the interview room steamed. Why did people think rain was cold?

Detective Carman listened to my information. "Yeah, we could send the apple to Sacramento, but we wouldn't have results from the Department of Justice for two or three weeks. It's pretty much take a number and wait." He smiled. "Are you suggesting we look for oleander, again?"

So he did know that I'd made the anonymous call. He realized his error too late. "How'd you know?" I asked.

"That boss of yours…the big, puffy guy?"

"Eldon," I supplied.

"Yes, Eldon mentioned that he'd seen you making a call, acting 'shifty.' I put two and two together, listened to the voice on the recording, and guessed." He seemed proud of his deductions.

With or without the tox-screen results, the apple episode had made me realize how unlikely it was that someone had doctored the honey in the kitchen. Just as no one had sneaked into the bakery and injected the apple with poison, no one would have popped the top on some honey, fussed with mixing oleander into the resistant goo, and tried to put everything back to normal in a busy, gossipy kitchen. I had not even been able to call the tip line without being spotted. The jar had been delivered for Fortier with the poison in it. I believed I knew who the murderer was and the motive.

As the rain outside slowed to a trickle, I shared my hypothesis with Detective Carman.

He listened patiently. When I'd finished, he thought about it, nodded, and said, "That's possible. Do you have any proof?"

The big question for me was did I want to prove it.

CHAPTER FORTY-ONE

I'd never been a fan of big holidays like Thanksgiving and Christmas. I prefer less crowded occasions—the Harvest Moon, the equinoxes, and January sixth, the last day of Christmas, the day of the wise men's arrival, the Epiphany.

On the way to work, I sang along with Tom Petty. By January sixth, Christmas sales ended, frantic lines to exchange gifts melted, and Archibald's removed the poisonous poinsettias (a four, according to *Deadly Doses*) along its staircase.

Petty sang about his lucky sister marrying a yuppie and taking him for all he was worth. I had the volume loud so I couldn't hear myself sing, an area in which I am remarkably untalented.

From the lot to Archibald's, I continued to sing, but softly, blotting my voice with the jingling rhythm of my keys. I walked in the middle of the road, away from trees and shrubs. Once inside, I turned on lights everywhere before I changed my clothes. I sucked on my sore lip and poked on my cheek to test its tenderness.

Today I was going to bake sesame brioche. I unlocked the refrigerator and crossed to my shelf. The foil cover on one bucket had been knocked off, probably by a cook shoving it aside to clear room for half-used products. My good mood vanished. I'd complain more emphatically. This was the bakery's shelf and I took pains to keep it neat and uncluttered.

I lifted the bucket. Droplets spattered the dough like dirty rain. I turned back to the Use-First shelf above mine. A covered, but raw piece of meat swam in blood. Surface tension amazingly held the red pool in the shallow plate, but even as I watched, a drop escaped, ran a circuitous route around the bottom, and finally let go. If I even breathed on the plate, I'd cause a spill, but I had to see the exact nature of this idiocy. I considered letting the blood spill through the racks to the floor and then insisting to Eldon that the culprit clean it. Somehow sweetness and light prevailed over my black spirit. I stepped out to the garde manger and nabbed one of their towels. I spread it where my bucket had been and carefully lifted the plastic over the meat. Blood sloshed over the edge of the plate.

Under the covering was a heart. A big heart. I jiggled the plate to spill more blood and then, carefully, drew down the platter.

The door opened, the seals sucking air, and I dropped the plate, spraying my shoes, pants and the floor with red. I bobbled a slippery heart, my hands coated with blood.

"I see you have a heart," Buzz said.

"Very funny." I picked up the empty plate while hanging on to the slick purplish organ with one hand. A smooth slice had flattened one side. I placed that side down on the plate and sat the raw meat on the shelf. "Blood from that thing dripped on my brioche dough." I wiped my hands on my smock since it was already streaked with red.

"That's the kind of stuff I've had to deal with, with Ray on the lead line."

"What kind of heart is it?"

"Beef. What did you think?"

Buzz poked through containers that had invaded my shelf.

"What's it doing here?"

"We had that movie star last night." Buzz glanced over his shoulder. "Michael What's his name? Some manager or secretary called ahead and said he wanted heart. For the iron."

"I thought people ate liver for iron." I snatched the already bloodied towel from my shelf and used it to mop blood from my shoes and the floor.

"That's what Eldon asked the secretary: 'Don't you mean liver?' The guy goes, 'No, he doesn't eat liver. Livers strain toxins and should never be eaten.'" Buzz shrugged and opened a large, green plastic bowl. "This is so goddamn frustrating."

"Whatcha looking for?"

"Chicken stock. For the curry. You can see how Ray puts stuff away, and he doesn't label a friggin' thing."

Buzz didn't have any right to complain. He and Eldon controlled the keys and should have managed the storage.

Buzz pulled forward a gallon jar. "Here it is." He walked toward the door, but I stomped out in front of him. I wasn't going to clean any more of the mess. The cooks were responsible and I wanted him to know it. I went to change my uniform.

Two minutes later, I bolted from the locker room, buttoning

my clean smock, an epiphany before my eyes. I hadn't locked the refrigerator because Buzz was there, and I bet he hadn't locked it because he expected me to return for the dough. Someone was waiting for this moment. With the door unlocked and Buzz and me in our niches, anybody could now enter the refrigerator. And someone desperately wanted to because that's where the honey was.

People had seen Fortier with the honey. He'd taken it into the refrigerator with him and I saw now with blinding clarity that it had never come out. Fortier had abandoned it there, possibly for another rendezvous with Delores.

The refrigerator was a natural place. A place where a jar would blend with the surroundings. Like the purloined letter, right in front of our eyes. *Well, not quite.*

To find it, I needed to do more than shove around the half-used quart of chutney, the wrapped wheel of cheese, and the white five-gallon buckets of pickles like the police must have done.

I entered the kitchen through the swinging door, grabbed my rolling pin from the bakery, and flew toward Buzz.

He saw the weapon and threw up his arms. "I promise I'll make Ray clean the shelf," he said.

I put a finger to my lips, but he continued. "My thigh has a bruise on it the size of a baseball, Carol."

"Did you lock the 'frig?" I whispered.

He shook his head and slowly lowered his hands.

"Did you hear someone go in there?"

"I might've, but I assumed it was you."

I crooked my finger and he followed me, wiping his fingers on a towel. I pulled open the refrigerator door.

"*¿Que estan haciendo ahora*?"

"We could ask you the same question," I said. "What are you doing?"

Victor stood with a great deal of dignity in the center of the cold cell, clutching a cheap ice chest to his stomach. He smiled. "Busted."

"What's in the cooler?" Buzz asked.

Victor sat the white box on the floor and squeaked off the lid. In it, ice cubes surrounded a large, white package.

Hanging his towel on my shelf, Buzz wiggled the package from the container, spilling ice cubes on to the tile. "Beef tender?"

"A farewell party," Victor said. "I guess that's going to be sooner than we expected."

"Probably."

"Have you found the honey?" Victor asked.

"Not yet. But I know where it is."

"Put back the meat," Buzz said.

He nodded. "I knew you'd figure it out, Carol."

CHAPTER FORTY-TWO

Victor left, toting his now empty ice chest. He didn't ask if we'd tell about his attempted theft. Either he knew we wouldn't, or he assumed he couldn't do anything about it if we did.

"How did you know Victor would be in here?" Buzz asked.

"I didn't. That's not what I expected at all."

The Use-First shelf was at shoulder height for me. I sat down the rolling pin and shoved aside containers.

"Carol, I told you I'd have Ray clean that."

I squatted and peered up through the wire shelf. I pulled off my chef's smock and rolled up my sleeves.

"Today," Buzz added.

"Help me."

"Help you what?"

I pushed a five-gallon, white bucket full of dill pickles to the edge of the shelf. "Lift this down to my shelf."

"You want me to put junk on your shelf?"

"Come on, Buzz. This is no time to joke around."

He hoisted down the heavy bucket. "What is it time for, Carol?" I handed him one of Ray's unlabeled, plastic, mystery containers.

While he held it, I pried open the lid. Inside was what looked like a squash puree. I stuck my hand into the goop. "Nope. Not here." I grabbed Buzz's towel from my shelf, wiped my hand and reached up again.

My arm froze. This was silly. Fortier wouldn't want to get dirty to retrieve his honey. I tapped my lip and inspected the containers. At the end of the shelf sat a gallon glass jar filled with a Cajun-spiced cornmeal mix. It didn't need to be in the refrigerator except that grains could hatch weevils and the cold decreased the possibility. This cornmeal was Fortier's special blend, something the other chefs wouldn't dare touch. And the meal would shake cleanly away from the jar.

Excited, I crossed the room and lifted down the jar.

Buzz set the plastic container on my shelf and held the heavy jar for me. I screwed off the lid, plunged my arm into the cornmeal, and fished for the prize. I pulled up a jar dripping golden grains. A puckered Christmas lick-and-stick tag clung to the red and white ribbon around the jar's neck. I read: To: My honey. From: Your honey. The penmanship was feminine and tentative.

The door sucked open.

"You did find it," Victor said, as though he had to see the fact to believe it. "Ever since you came to the house, I knew you would. You were like a woman possessed."

Buzz shot me a look.

"You know about that?" I asked Victor.

He rolled his eyes to the ceiling. "I'm the one who had to tell The Kid our *visitor* wasn't Suzanne."

His gaze returned to our eyes. It held a silent plea.

I quite seriously considered becoming an accessory to murder. When I looked at Buzz, I could tell he was also thinking about it. I supposed we already were accessories having allowed Victor time to make a phone call, although, I rationalized, at that moment I had not yet found the evidence.

I sucked on my lip. "She hit me, Victor."

"I am very sorry about that, Carol." He looked contrite. "She probably thought she could get that honey, as long as you didn't find it, but she got scared with you coming in here every day."

"You knew all this time?"

"I wondered. Ever since that *puto* got my honey."

"Why didn't you take the honey just now?"

"Oh, I am not as clever as you, Carol. I didn't know it was here."

Of course not, I thought, but Esperanza did because she knew exactly the type of thing Fortier would do. Maybe Delores had even told her. "Why did she kill him?"

Victor shrugged. "You can't tell your kids who to like. They jus' hate you. I think Delores loved the *puto*. But like a father. He shoulda been her stepfather. Instead he gave Esperanza money and said, 'Get an abortion.' Well she did," Victor said. "I am ashamed I didn't kill him then. He still came around. I couldn't believe it. Finally, I put a knife to his throat and he got the message. When he got with Delores, it felt sick. He used to play with her, take her on the swings."

I tightened my grip on the jar and picked up the rolling pin.

With Buzz there, it seemed unlikely Victor would lunge for the jar, but I wasn't about to end up with another fat lip. "Victor, this is a tough decision for me, but Esperanza will need a good lawyer."

"Delores was the only baby Esperanza had left," Victor said, "and Fortier was going to kill her. In the heart." He clasped the left side of his chest as though it ached.

"I have to call the police, Victor."

He smiled. He knew that I knew he had made a phone call, a secret we could never speak. With his knowledge of safe houses, in ten hours or so, Esperanza would disappear into Mexico.

"It's what you have to do, Carol."

CHAPTER FORTY-THREE

Chad and I sat on the back steps. Lola napped in the crushed Peruvian lilies. I held Chad's hand, but the way his foot jiggled told me that he needed his nicotine fix. This probably wasn't a good time to talk. But it had taken weeks for me to gather the courage, and I felt ready now.

"Chad, what would you think if I decided to make a career change?"

"And become a cop?" His voice was almost surly and he retracted his hand.

"No. I'm a little old for that."

He patted the pocket of his flannel shirt.

"They're on the table," I said.

He ignored this. "Let's see. Not a cop, then a private investigator?"

"Sorta."

"Sorta?" He stood. The yard was too small for pacing. He

looked through the sliding glass door to his package of Vantage on the table.

"Remember how I mentioned Rat Dog? She traces down deadbeat dads? Maybe I could do work like that. Not too dangerous."

"The way this case was 'not too dangerous'?"

"Esperanza wouldn't have killed me."

"She killed Fortier."

That was the bottom line. Poisoned him. I remembered that summer afternoon with Patsy and Suzanne. The memory stirred up guilt the way nudging beached seaweed stirred up gnats. Had my glib holding forth trickled back to the kitchen? Both Suzanne and Patsy loved to gab. Had I inadvertently planted the idea for murder in Esperanza's head? Had she taken my book *Deadly Doses* out of my locker and leafed through it for ideas? Doubt and fear swarmed around me, thick, but amorphous. I couldn't bat away the feelings, but I wasn't ready, yet, to voice them. Clearly, though, I needed some productive way to use the plotting, dark part of my character, so that it didn't spill uncontrollably into harm.

As though he sensed my emotional turmoil, Chad sat and took my hand again. "Do you think they'll catch Esperanza?"

I shook my head. "No. But she may never see Delores, or Victor, or Abundio. She's lost the most important thing in her life—her family."

"But she saved her daughter. Her motivation was noble," he said. "Not like greed or revenge." He rose and stretched. "Speaking of noble, I'm going to see a hypnotist."

Inwardly I applauded, but I didn't say anything on the off chance that he meant to see a hypnotist for a reason other than to stop smoking. He kept stretching elaborately, as though warming up for a big event.

"I would have tried hypnotism before, but I hate the idea of losing control of myself."

"If you pick someone reputable, I don't think you have to worry. He won't make you oink like a pig or anything."

"It's not that," Chad said with irritation.

Enough irritation that I almost wanted him to go take a puff.

All right, it wasn't that, so what was it? He didn't want to lose control. That was understandable given what had happened to him when he was little, given what his life had been like when he didn't control it. I took a deep breath.

"Sorry." I wished my mother were present to witness the moment. She would have collapsed on top of Lola in the flowerbed. Sorry was a rare word in my lexicon.

Chad smiled grimly.

I could see now that the topic of the conversation hadn't really changed. Indirectly, we had been discussing control the whole time. In his own way, Chad was apologizing for needing to control me, for not letting me go, not encouraging a career change.

And, for once, with the smoking, I had backed off, released my control, letting him find a solution. I wondered, sadly, if Buzz would find one.

I clapped. "I'm so glad you're going to try this, Chad!" One hurdle at a time, I figured. I had a lot of practical stuff to sort through before I could make a career change.

Chad glanced toward the cigarettes on the table and then sat back on the steps. "So what happened with Suzanne and Eldon?"

He switched to this lighter subject to keep himself from the cellophane packet.

"Well," I said with enthusiasm, "Suzanne asked Eldon for days off."

"Days off! Whoa! But from what you've told me, wouldn't he just give them to her."

"Oh, he did."

"So, what's the punch line?"

"Suzanne told him she needed the time because her herpes were flaring up. She figured that would discourage his interest."

We laughed together for the first time in weeks. It felt good.

###

If you enjoyed this book, please consider writing a review on Amazon. If you let me know about it via e-mail: vinnie@vinniehansen.com, I will send you a free trade paper copy of another Carol Sabala mystery.

LEBKUCHEN

Unlike Carol Sabala, most of us do not have a professional bakery at our fingertips. Lebkuchen is not as easy to whip up as chocolate chip cookies. A person needs to be motived. For me, the motivation is love of a good spice cookie.

Here's my recipe, a modification from Betty Crocker since I don't like things as sweet as most recipes dictate, because I couldn't find citron in April when I went to make the lebkuchen, (I'm sure it would be more available during the Christmas, fruitcake-baking season), and because I didn't have any allspice. You get the idea. It's not really Betty Crocker at all! I also use organic ingredients as much as possible.

3/8 cup honey
1/2 cup black strap molasses
3/4 cup brown sugar
1 egg
1 tsp. grated lemon peel
1 tbsp. lemon juice
2 ¾ cups all-purpose flour
1 tsp. each of cinnamon, cloves and nutmeg
1/2 tsp. soda
2 tbsp. dried orange peel, dampened ahead of time to render soft so you don't break anyone's tooth!
1/3 cup chopped walnuts

Optional icing: I used my mom's simple powder sugar/milk mix to create a thin icing to brush across the cookies. If you've never made this icing, start with 1/2 cup powdered sugar and add the tiniest dab of milk to it. Stir until all lumps are dissolved. Add miniscule amounts of milk until you have a glaze. Remember that the icing will continue to melt/thin on top the warm cookie.

Combine the honey and molasses in a saucepan and heat to boiling. Cool. Stir in sugar, egg, lemon peel and juice. Mix in the other ingredients and chill for at least 8 hours.

Heat oven to 400. For one sheet of cookies, scoop about 1/3 of the dough onto a lightly floured board. Keep the remaining dough refrigerated. With a lightly floured rolling pin, roll the dough to 1/4 inch thick. Cut with cookie cutters. Place 1 inch apart on greased baking sheet. Bake 10 to 12 minutes.

Remove from baking sheet. Ice while warm. Cool and store in an airtight container with a slice of orange. Makes 3-5 dozen, depending on the cookie cutter size.

ACKNOWLEDGMENTS

I owe thanks to many people: Sergeant Joe Haebe of the Santa Cruz Police Department; Dr. Mason, Santa Cruz County Coroner; the members of my writing group—Sharlya Gold, Erica Lann-Clark, and Bob O'Brien—to my former chef husband Malcolm for knowledge of a kitchen.

Many others have read and commented on the manuscript: my mom Vivian Hansen, my sister and brother-in-law Carol and Al Vogan, my colleague Nanci Adams, and my fellow murder mystery writer Genny Obert. Thanks to Rich Cowan for the skull and crossbones on the original cover, to Kimiye Welch and Justin Owens for their on-going computer assistance, to Herb Jellinek for his careful proofreading, and to Joan Fenwick for a final read through.

Most of all, thanks to misterio press!

ABOUT THE AUTHOR

Vinnie Hansen is the author of the Carol Sabala mystery series: *Murder, Honey*; *One Tough Cookie*; *Rotten Dates*; *Tang Is Not Juice*; *Death with Dessert;* and *Art, Wine & Bullets.* She was a Claymore Award finalist for her upcoming Carol Sabala mystery, *Black Beans & Venom.* A semi-finalist for the Iowa School of Letters Award for Short Fiction, she has written many published short stories. Vinnie lives in Santa Cruz, California, with her husband, abstract artist Daniel S. Friedman. Please visit her website at http://vinniehansen.com. She's also on Facebook and Goodreads.

VINNIEHANSEN.COM

49827670R00132

Made in the USA
Charleston, SC
04 December 2015